ASIMOV'S LAWS

Gordon A. Long

Delta, B. C.
2020

Asimov's Laws

Gordon A. Long

Published by

AIRBORN PRESS

4958 10A Ave, Delta, B. C.

V4M 1X8

Canada

ISBN: 978-1-988898-23-0

Printed by Amazon

Cover Design by Gordon A. Long
Cover image by Gerd Altmann
https://pixabay.com/users/geralt-9301/

TOO-POWERFUL ALLIES

At the sound of Toni's footsteps the two guards had retreated right where she predicted, a huge room with a warren of aisles of shelving. She paused outside, calling Andrew's augment.

I'm going in. Is there anything you can do about those damn barwolves? They're putting constant pressure on me now.

What do you mean, pressure?

They want to join my gestalt with Nzinga. It's a real distraction, like static on a com system. Can you get them off my back?

I'll work on it.

She registered her opponents on the VR map and moved into the intersecting corridors, sending Nzinga in a flanking movement. A plan was coming together in her head.

Then one of the guards disappeared.

Crap. A heat shield. This one's a pro. Have to be careful.

She kept his last known position in her mind and moved. The tension was rising. The adrenaline rush before the final clash.

But the pressure from the barwolves was building, too.

Emotion: desire to join the pack.

Emotion: negative.

Emotion: strong desire to join. Pleading to join.

Emotion: NO! You can't help! Calm do...

She was brought back to re-ti by a rush of soft footsteps behind her, and before she could refocus and turn, an arm slipped around her neck. She grabbed, feeling corded muscles as the wrist slid over the collar of her flak vest into the perfect position for a chokehold impossible to break.

She lashed back with her heel and missed. She drove her elbow into a stomach that felt like concrete.

Nzinga...

Emotion: helpless rush. Image: auguar frantically dodging around corners, down alleys.

Her vision was narrowing, darkness closing in on her...

CONTENTS

If you look at something and assume you understand it, you will only see evidence that confirms your opinion.

...Morissa Goodall

PROLOGUE

Nzinga did not understand. *The Pride Leader is angry, so angry. M'dora-cat is very worried. Corporal Ito is so frightened she cannot move.* The young auguar tried to peer into the darkness of the alley, but could see nothing but a jumble of human figures.

The hairs rose on the big cat's neck. *It is those ugly, smelly humans.*

Emotion: question? Emotion: growing anger!

Emotion: calmness. I can handle this, little one. Pride Leader slipped silently into the darkness, and Nzinga shadowed Her.

Emotion: uncertainty.

The Pride Leader laid a calming hand on her head. *They are not nice people, Nzinga. They want to hurt Ito. I will not allow it.*

Emotions: relief, uncertainty.

The leader made the hand signal to stay and stepped forward, raising Her voice with authority. "Just what's going on, here?"

The largest of the three men turned away from his victim. "Well, whaddaya know? It's another little pussy-lover. Have you come to join the party, sweetheart?"

Odours: alcohol, sweat, human lust.

Nzinga bared her teeth in a silent snarl.

Pride Leader slipped into a lower stance, Her feet gripping the dirty pavement. "That's what I thought was going on. And now it's not." She stepped aside. "Move along, all three of you."

The other two turned to face Her as well. They were big men, topping the two small auguar trainers by a full head. "Oh, no, sweetheart. We just want some information from your kitty friend here, and maybe a little entertainment, as well." The leader stepped forward, towering over Her. "Why don't you come on in?"

Emotion: concern.

Stay there, Nzinga. You must not attack a human unless I say so. Understand?

Emotion: compliance, trust.

Corporal Ito, move around to your left. Bring M'dora to heel and keep him under control. Do you read me?

Emotion: compliance.

M'dora?

Emotion: fear, growing anger.

M'dora, you will do as you are ordered. This is a test of your obedience.

Emotion: reluctant compliance.

Emotion: complete dominance! Nzinga's glare bored into the smaller cat's eyes. *She sent a rapid series of images and emotions that shouted,* "The Pride Leader has given you an order. This is human business, and She will handle it. YOU WILL COMPLY!"

Emotion: abject compliance. The smaller auguar tucked in safely at his trainer's side, staring around in fear of the men and of the Prime Cat's displeasure.

The leading human stepped forward. "Well, don't just stand there staring like a dummy." His leer showed a broken tooth. "Get over here by your friend and let's get to it..."

Ito, now!

...hey! I didn't say you could move..."

The moment his attention turned to the other woman, the Pride Leader attacked, taking the enemy down with a kick to the side of his knee and spinning him to drive a forearm into his throat as he fell. The other two piled onto her, raining fists against her exposed back, but she tore free and faced them, dodging and weaving, making her blows count.

Ito, M'dora. Run!

Emotion: uncertainty, rising panic

I can handle this. Run! Nzinga, hold there.

Emotion: fear, anger.

No, Nzinga. No anger. Stay!

As the other handler and her auguar tore away, the Pride Leader disengaged from the two thugs. They stood, panting, blood dripping from battered faces.

She gestured to the ground. "Your buddy is in bad shape. You need to get him to the hospital before his throat swells up and he can't breathe at all. Move!"

The last word was blasted at them with the power of a drill sergeant's shout, and they obeyed, hoisting their companion's arms over their shoulders and dragging him away.

The Pride Leader stood, watching them go.

Emotion: satisfaction. Well done, Nzinga. You held firm in a tough situation. You're a very brave auguar. Now let's make sure the others are all right.

She turned to follow Ito, and Nzinga paced beside her.

Emotion: pride and relief. Nzinga accessed their gestalt to read the Leader's condition. *Emotion: concern.*

Just a few bruises. Come on. We have to get these two home before they fall apart. We also have to get out of this neighbourhood in case those assholes think to bring reinforcements.

The Pride Leader thought as she walked. *Hmm. Those men fought like trained soldiers. That puts a different slant on things...*

1. GETTING THE BOOT

The expected debrief came early the next morning. Toni stood at the doorway scanning General Greer's office. *Looks more like a mad scientist's lab than an officer's workroom.* But the general knew how to use every one of those machines and had invented a couple of them himself. *A scientist first, a general second.*

"Come in, Jacobs." Greer returned her salute and motioned her to take a chair. "Now, what's this I hear about a brawl with common soldiers?"

She considered her response. "Is that what you think it was, sir?"

He sighed. "No, that's what the official report by the MPs says it was. I think Ito got herself in trouble and you went in and pulled her out in your usual forthright manner. By beating someone up." He glanced at his viewscreen. "Three of them."

She nodded. "That would be an accurate, if simplified, view of the incident."

He frowned. "Simplified? You mean there was more to it than a sexual assault by drunk soldiers?"

"There was mention of gaining information, sir. The rape attempt was a screen. They were after more."

"I was afraid of that." He sighed. "This is the part of my job I don't like. Now I have to cover up the whole situation. Why couldn't you have handled it with a bit more..." a vague wave of his hand, "...discretion?"

"Discretion?" She stood. "One of my cohort was about to be tortured in a particularly nasty way for information about our program. Her auguar was on the verge of breaking his training and attacking a human without permission. Can you picture what you'd be trying to hide if I hadn't acted as I did?"

"I don't know. I can't help but wonder why you didn't call for help. That's what augments are for..." He made a placating gesture. "No, no, I wasn't there. I can't second-guess your decisions. You're a Commando, you reacted as your training led you to and the short-term results were satisfactory. Nobody dead, nobody hurt that doesn't deserve it." He glanced at her. "You didn't report to the hospital. Aren't you injured?"

"Nothing worse than a tough training session might produce."

He rested his elbows on his desk, his chin on his interlaced fingers. "Jacobs, I'm still not certain why they seconded you for this project. You are simply too violent in nature for such delicate work."

"With all respect to your position, sir, I feel I am exactly violent enough for my work. And may I draw your attention to the opinions of my superiors for the past five years, who think the same."

"But those are Commandos, not scientists!"

"That's right, sir. And when Nzinga and I are finished our training, I assume we will be placed in a Commando troop where the wrong attitude towards violence would be a detriment to the safety of our fellow spacers."

"There will come a time when none of that is necessary."

"I hope it will come soon, sir. But until it does, I will continue to do my best to serve and protect humankind, as I swore in my oath when I joined the Space Arm."

The general shook his head. "Nobody can say you don't do your best, Second Lieutenant. But it's all out of my hands now, anyway."

"It is?"

"I no longer have jurisdiction over you, so this latest incident has no significance. You seem to have friends in high places, and you're being transferred."

Toni stared at the general, frowning. "I'm sorry, sir, but you've completely left me behind. I have no idea what you're talking about. What friends?"

He raised his eyebrows. "Do you deny your contacts in the Diplomatic Corps? You mean to tell me you didn't call them up to get you out of this mess?"

Toni snapped to attention. "Sir. I do not consider this situation a mess. My actions were completely in keeping with my duty and

5

my conscience. I will stake my career and my reputation on that fact, and I need no help from anyone to defend myself!"

General Greer sighed. "At ease, Lieutenant. That is a melodramatic and rather naïve statement, and given the present circumstances, rather pointless." He stood, an envelope in his hand. "Orders have come through unusual channels. You and your auguar are to be graduated forthwith from this training program, and you will be promoted to full Lieutenant. You will return to Commando Headquarters to await transport to your assignment."

Promotion? New assignment? She stayed calm. "Which will be...?"

He shrugged. "I don't think there's much doubt. The only place the Commandos are active at the moment is in the Barnard System."

A bolt of pleasure shot through her, but she kept her face stoic, saving her emotions for an augment message. *Nzinga, you're going to meet the great Chakka!*

Image: small cub adoring huge male auguar.

Don't worry, Pumpkin. He's just a big pussycat. I'll be finished here in a moment. Stay there.

Emotion: compliance.

"Toni, I don't like this situation. We are creating a new type of military force, here, and we have by no means finished its development. Your input, abrasive though it may be, has been invaluable in forming the organization we wish to create. However, we are at a delicate stage in our progress, and any unfavourable publicity or negative feedback from other departments could have adverse effects. We are not without our detractors and competitors."

He shook his head. "I am sending you and your auguar out into the general forces with great trepidation."

She put on a gentle smile. "General, I can allay most of those fears. While I may not have fit into this scientific milieu smoothly, in the Commandos I disappear completely. I'm one of the rank and file. One of the followers. I only stood out because of being good at my duties in a completely traditional way, and I only ended up here because of my luck in being assigned to Captain O'Rourke and Chakka and due to the missions we were sent on."

He shook his head again with a wry grin. "I think you will find that a rather difficult role to slip back into. However, I know what you mean." He shrugged. "I suppose I should be happy."

"Why?"

"Because I had to lose one of my teams to fill the post you have been given. Like Chakka, the auguar who is assigned to work with Andrew Collingwood will no longer fit in our program once the mission is complete."

"Right. You are trying to keep this a pure Space Arm project to prevent coming under the influence of Factory 4-80. So Nzinga and I will be contaminated, and since we never fit into your program, that suits you."

He tilted his head left, then right. "To some extent that is true, harsh though it may sound." He threw up his hands. "Don't get me wrong, Toni. I like you. You're a strong, intelligent person with her head screwed on right. It's just your casual attitude towards violence that frightens me. You were almost raped, and it doesn't seem to have affected you at all."

"Oh, I don't think there was much chance of that."

"You don't? There were three of them."

She levelled him a stare. "And the only thing that saved them was my reluctance to expose Nzinga to violence against humans at this stage of her development. Do you think I ever go off base without my knife?"

He sat straighter, his eyebrows rising. Then he nodded slowly, his mind processing.

She leaned forward, her knuckles on the desk. "And I'll leave you with a thought that arises from this situation, sir. A lot of my actions last night were aimed at keeping our auguars from attacking humans before they had been thoroughly prepared. How much do Asimov's Laws of Robotics apply to auguars?"

"Asimov." He knitted his fingers together under his chin. "Once again you prove your worth to the program. Asimov's laws

7

have been discussed in a theoretical sense, but until now we had no practical reason to apply them. Chakka is the only auguar on active duty, and I have no idea how Captain O'Rourke handles that aspect of his training. After this incident, I will be expecting lively debate on the topic."

"There needs to be. When you say, 'active duty,' you know what that means, don't you?"

"I assume so. He has attacked humans?"

"He was an invaluable asset in several actions, sir."

He nodded, his mind on something else. Then he straightened and laid his hands flat on the desk. "I have changed my mind, Lieutenant Jacobs. It would be foolish of me to sever connections with such valuable personnel as yourself. You will no longer fit in our program, but that does not prevent you from having input. May I send you away with an unofficial assignment?"

"Anything I can do to help, sir." She grinned. "I remember a comment Ensign Collingwood made once. He said it's best to leave your old job on a happy note. You might want it back some day."

"The same applies to an ex-employee. Out there where the ordnance is live, please keep Asimov's laws in mind. A person in your position is much more likely to experience their application."

She shrugged. "That's an easy one, sir. If we're working with Andrew and Chakka, I can hardly help but consider that element of our training. I'll write up our findings for you."

He stood and held out his hand. "That makes me feel better, Toni. This is not the end of our association, but merely a new branch to our program."

She shook his hand, giving him a wry grin. "I'm not so unhappy about it, myself. It makes it feel less like I got kicked out on my ass."

He tilted his head to one side. "Yes, I thought of that, too." Then he saluted. "Best of luck in your new assignment, Lieutenant. I expect to hear from you."

"Aye, sir. I'll be in touch." She saluted, did a proper about face and strode out.

Nzinga was busy entertaining the general's secretary but twisted to her feet the moment Toni entered the office.

Emotion: guilt.

Emotion: glee. Don't worry, Pumpkin. A bit of public relations never hurts. Let's go pack our bags. We're headed for action!

"Hey, Lieutenant Jacobs, what have you been doing with your spare time?"

Toni looked up from the lounger where she sat grooming Nzinga's left front paw. "I don't have anything but spare time, right now. What are you talking about?"

The Commando corporal poked a thumb over his shoulder. "You better get to the viewscreen in the common room and tell us."

"The viewscreen? What is this, some kind of a joke?"

"Must be. Micha the Mouse is on the screen and he's asking for you."

She shot to her feet. "What?"

"That's right. Micha the Mouse. He's interrupted the Rose Bowl game and he's hogging all the other channels."

"I've got it, Corporal." With a pat to her auguar's head, she strode out the door. "Come on, girl. You're about to meet an old friend of mine."

When she reached the common room, a large crowd had gathered around the entertainment module. Three commandos were deep in conversation with the toon on the screen, and as she approached, a roar of laughter went up. Then the crowd parted, and she strode through.

"Toni! At last I have found you."

Silence descended on the room; all eyes turned her way.

She took a pose, hands on hips. "Mouse. Do you realize you're keeping these people from the Rose Bowl game?"

"Yes, well, I'm sorry about that, but I couldn't find you anywhere. Don't you people ever watch your entertainment media?"

"We don't have time for frivolities. Only important events like the Rose Bowl. Now, switch yourself to the screen in the visitors' lounge down the hall, and let these folks find out who's winning."

"I already told them. They don't believe me."

10

"You're wasting valuable game time, Mouse." She turned away. "See you there."

As she pushed out of the crowd, she waved away their questions. "Sorry about that, guys, I have fans all over the place. You know how it is."

They laughed, but then the roar of the football crowd grabbed their attention.

The visitors' lounge was empty except for the image on the viewscreen, where Micha the Mouse, in an old-fashioned leather football helmet, was making a touchdown against a team of huge bulldogs with spiked collars poking out from under their helmets.

"Hey, Freighty. Good to see you. What's up?"

The toon turned from his end-zone celebrations and stood, hands on hips, to regard her. "Looking good, Jacobs. Full Lieutenant, I see. And this is the famous Nzinga?"

Emotion: feline humour. Image: Good cub being careful not to eat small, tasty mouse.

"That's right, girl. He's a friend, no matter what he looks like. So, what's up?"

"Your next assignment is what's up. What are you doing with yourself, right now?"

Toni considered her response, remembering the conversations she had heard between Captain O'Rourke and the avatar. "Dare I guess that you know exactly what we're doing? As in holding ourselves ready for our next assignment, which I'm sure you know all about?"

Micha sat in a dejected slouch. "Here I am, trying the deft touch, and all I get is abuse."

"Right. And now that we've been through the social niceties, can we get down to the business we came for?"

The avatar frowned. "Are all women of your species like this, or was I just unlucky to get tied up with you and Natalia?"

She merely stared at him, her fingers playing in the orange patches of Nzinga's fur.

11

"All right, all right. Your assignment. We need you out here. The barwolves are turning out to be more trouble than they're worth, and Ambassador Pretoro has asked for help to deal with them downplanet."

"That sounds interesting, but Nzinga is still very young and just out of training. We didn't even get finished, as you well know."

"And who was the dominant female in the whole program?"

Toni shrugged. "Not unexpected. I was the most experienced handler."

"Sorry, kid. You can't take all the credit. She's the Alpha kitten in the pride, and her augment is pure organic. We need that kind of help to keep these barwolves from tearing each other to shreds."

"Right. And you took all my metallic augments out last year when we visited on our way back to Earth." She frowned suspiciously. "Were you grooming me for this position?"

"Precisely. How's your augment progressing?"

"In leaps and bounds and falling flat on my face once a week, thank you very much. The biotechs at the hospital have had a field day. They're quite miffed their primary source of new data is being removed."

"Couldn't be helped. We want you out here as quickly as transport will allow. We're looking at possibilities. Be ready for space in the next couple of weeks."

"Whatever you say, Freighty. You're pulling all the strings."

"I'm finding it much more useful to let you humans pull your own strings. You've got ever so much more practice at it. Ta-ta for now."

His clothing morphed into tuxedo and top hat, and he bowed, tossing a bouquet of flowers at the screen as he faded away.

* * *

It took a couple of days for Toni to tie up loose ends in the Feline Augment program and tidy her business affairs. The third day she ran out of entertainment in the middle of the afternoon and found it hard to occupy herself until a decent time before heading for a beer.

Picking up her drink from the dispenser, she looked around the Commandos' lounge. It was a barren room, with tough, simple furniture and a huge PermaPlex viewscreen, which this afternoon was broadcasting an Augmented Mixed Martial Arts bout, to the great delight of half a dozen young Commandos who cheered and jeered the participants in equal amounts.

She brought her beer over to a table in a quieter corner where two other female Commandos were sitting. "Mind if I join you?"

The blonde looked up. "Feel free. You're Jacobs, right? The one with the pretty pet?"

"You mean the one in the corner behind you?" She glanced down at Nzinga, curled in a large ball of white, orange and black spots so furry that only the two ears perking out showed which end was which. "I think she's pretty."

The second woman raised her eyebrows. "Pretty quiet. I never even saw her there."

The first nudged her larger friend. "A lot of the guys would love a chance to pet her, that's for sure."

Toni frowned. "By which you mean...?"

The darker woman laughed. "Don't mind Sarah. She's just broke up with her latest and she's looking around. Thus, she assumes we're all feeling the same way. Which we aren't, especially with our fellow Commandos." She reached out a muscular leg and kicked a chair in Toni's direction. "I'm Jamie Patrick. Weapons Specialist. Welcome."

Toni took the chair. "Right up my alley, second only to Infiltration and Barehand."

"I noticed you around the past couple of days. Who you attached to?"

"Nobody. I'm waiting for transport to my next assignment."

"Any idea where? Or can you say?"

13

Toni shrugged. "No specific orders, but probably better if I don't." She took a pull from her beer. "Sort of boring. Nothing to do for a couple of weeks."

"Well, come around for a chat during training hours. Anyone's welcome. Always possible to learn a new trick from a stranger, and word has it you know some tricks."

Sarah chimed in with a comment about a new sidearm she was trying out, and the three women talked shop for a while. But then Toni's mind began to wander.

She leaned back and surveyed the room. "Is it just me, or is there a larger number of rather hot young bodies in here?"

Sarah elbowed her friend, "Hah! So it's not just me." She looked around. "No, I'd have to say it's also you. Looks like a run-of-the mill bunch of faces. Of course the bodies…well, they are Commandos, after all."

"Hmm." Toni shrugged. "Having nothing to do must be getting to me."

"Well, come out tomorrow at ten-thirty and we'll put you through your paces."

"Suits me fine. Anyone for another beer?"

"If it's on you, I can afford one." Jamie's broad brow wrinkled. "Ever notice that the cost of a beer in the canteen is exactly enough that you can afford one a night on a corporal's pay?"

"Well, I'm a big spender tonight, because for the next year or so I'm going somewhere I can't spend any money at all." She frowned at them. "And that's the last you're getting out of me."

"What, beer or information?"

"I'll leave that to you to figure out."

3. TAXI DRIVER

Her friendship with the two women developed, and they got in the habit of having a beer together every evening before dinner, when the lounge was quieter.

About a week later, Toni was early — she had no assignments to keep her busy— and she was sitting at their usual table, glancing now and then at some silly comedy on the viewscreen when she got a sudden prickling in her augment.

Warning: danger!

She jumped up and spun, ready to defend herself.

A huge male auguar, his pelt patterned like that of a cloud leopard, stalked towards her. A rumbling purr echoed off the walls of the lounge.

"Chakka!" She rushed forward and threw her arms around his neck, wrestling him to the floor. With a flip, he upended her, planting both front paws on her chest and rasping her face with his tongue. She laughed and grabbed his cheek hair with both hands, pushing him away.

Emotion: angry jealousy!

A bundle of speckled fur burst between them, shouldering the larger auguar aside. Disregarding her trainer's discomfort, Nzinga planted her bottom on Toni's stomach and one paw on each shoulder and stared down into her eyes. Then she swivelled her head to glare at Chakka.

Mine!

Emotion: feline laughter.

Emotion: feline puzzlement.

Emotion: human laughter.

Toni wrestled her cat off her and sat up.

A tall, broad-shouldered youth stood at her feet, slapping his thighs and roaring with glee. When he could compose himself, he shook his head. "Oh, if only you could have seen Chakka's face."

She reached up a hand. "Chakka's?"

He lifted her easily to her feet, his grip firm. "Yeah, when Nzinga knocked him flying. I told him to be polite. He should have listened."

She glanced down to where her auguar was pressed tightly against her knees, glaring up at Andrew. "Looks like you're getting the same message."

He met the auguar's eyes. *Emotion: dominance.*

Emotion: sulky compliance. She turned her head away and stared up at him from under wrinkled brows, her upper lip twitching.

He laughed again and reached out casually to pat her cheek.

Toni felt a bolt of fear. "Andrew…"

As the auguar opened her mouth to snatch at his hand he flipped his thumb down and inserted it behind her lower canines, grasping her jaw and twisting it to bring her face closer to his. *No!*

Nzinga's eyes widened until the whites showed. Her hind legs faltered, and her tail disappeared between them. Gradually she sank into a crouch.

He held her there a moment, then slowly released his hand, allowing his fingers to trail up and behind her ears, where he scratched gently.

"That's better. You've been lording it over everyone too much, young lady. You need to learn your place in this world."

Then he straightened and looked Toni up and down. "So, here we are. You're certainly looking good."

She found herself frowning. "What do you mean by that?"

He chuckled. "Don't tell me I have to go through the same rigamaroll with you. I just meant that you look good. You've grown your hair. Well, a little bit."

She shrugged and ran her fingers over the soft down on her scalp. "My old do was a little harsh for the lab environment."

He regarded her. "And it's not just that. You look…different." Then he shrugged. "Not important. How are you doing? This minx is keeping you busy, it seems. I read the reports."

Toni had the feeling that the conversation was completely out of her control. "Nice to see you, too, Andrew. I didn't know you were coming by."

His broad shoulders shrugged. "Stopped by Freighty on the way here. He tweaked *Diablo's* Otherwhere sphere a bit, and I was motivated to make a quick run. Tell you about that later."

"Well, that's great. What's the schedule? I mean, at the moment. Are you here for a while? Do you want a cola or something?"

"Sure. Let's sit down and gossip while the beasties are making acquaintance."

She looked down. Making acquaintance seemed to involve Chakka grooming his paws and Nzinga looking anywhere but at him.

Toni indicated a chair, and while he sat she went over to the machine and got them drinks. By the time she returned she had regained some of her poise. She looked at him, lounging in the chair, his long legs stretched out. "You're looking pretty good yourself, kid. Would it be insulting to mention that you've grown?"

He glanced down as if surprised. "Guess I did. Two years will do that to you when you're my age."

"You've kept up your training."

"Both *NightHawk* and *Diablo* have the power to run at full-G acceleration, so that keeps me exercised."

"Wait a minute. You said Freighty tweaked *Diablo's* engines. You didn't come all the way here in that rustbucket?"

"Sure. Freighty designed an external fuel tank that's literally twice the volume of the whole ship, and the old SolarCorp repair cadre fabricated it for me. *Diablo* sort of sits in it like a cat on a soft pillow. I leave it in orbit when I come downplanet."

"I see. And you're my ride back to Barnard's?"

"Seems that way. I had to make a run to bring a couple of diplomats back for R & R. You want my opinion — and I just spent four months in a small ship with them — neither of them

17

will be going back. Hence the quick trip here. I wanted to hit atmo before they killed each other."

She grinned. "But you expect me to spend three months plus in the same small ship with you. What makes you think we'll both survive?"

"In the opinion of Captain O'Rourke, you and I can handle a multitude of different circumstances. Do you want a chaperone? We've already got two." He nudged his shoe under Chakka's neck, and the big auguar rubbed against the laces.

Then a new voice broke in from behind her. "Oh, my gawd, would you look at this one. Jamie, look at this guy. He is just tooo beautiful."

Toni turned. "You better be talking about the auguar, girl, or there's going to be trouble."

Sarah had the grace to blush, but she soon recovered. "Then introduce us to your new boyfriend so there'll be no misunderstandings."

Andrew had risen to his feet as the two women approached, and now Jamie looked him up and down. "Choosing them a bit young, aren't you?"

Toni sighed. "Andrew, this disreputable pair is all I could find for friends in this place. Sarah Munis and Jamie Patrick. Ladies, this is Andrew Collingwood, an old shipmate of mine. Space Arm's foremost expert on organic augments." She frowned at them. "And the son of Commando Captain Natalia O'Rourke, a name you may be familiar with."

Jamie reached out to shake Andrew's hand. "Well, that would explain the auguar. There can't be too many like Chakka around. Everybody knows about him."

"Glad to meet you, ladies. Can I stand you a drink?"

Sarah glanced at his cola. "Don't think I'm up for that stuff so early in the evening. How about a beer?"

"Sure."

As he walked towards the bar, Sarah giggled. "Can he afford it out of his allowance?"

Jamie nudged her buddy. "Sarah, you fool, didn't you catch the last name?"

"What, Collingwood...? No. Not those Collingwoods..."

Toni nodded. "Afraid so, but don't bring it up. Touchy subject."

"Oh, sure enough. I can be cool." She nudged Toni's arm. "You're moving in elevated circles, girl."

"I sure am. And you're going to keep your mouth shut about it, because you're a Commando and you know the rules."

"Sure enough...oh, thanks, Andrew. Say, how did you know I drink Guinness?"

"Chakka accessed the till and checked your bar bill."

"No shit! I didn't know auguars could do that."

"They can't. He's been given some extra punch because of the duties he gets called for. Mum's into some pretty strange stuff, you know, and she needs all the help she can get."

Jamie frowned. "We hear hints on the Commando grapevine of Captain O'Rourke's escapades, but nobody says much. I thought it was all hush-hush."

He leaned back and took another sip of cola. "Nah, with all the news reports about the Rebellion we pretty much had to give the public something to chew on. I'm allowed to spill the official version, and that's it."

The two women leaned forward. "So, tell us the official version."

Toni listened carefully as well. *It would have been nice if someone had told me the official version.*

Emotion: apology. We only made it up because I was coming to Earth. Here's the file. You can check it over later.

She glanced at him. While communicating by augment he hadn't missed a beat in his story. She watched him as he talked. The extra height he had put on had thinned him out, giving his cheekbones definition. His uniform stretched across his shoulders, revealing the muscle rippling underneath.

He shot her a momentary glance and his brow furrowed, but then he was back to his story, telling it with an animation that kept the two older women rapt.

Toni clamped down on her augment fiercely. *He's only sixteen years old. What's wrong with me?*

There was a brief pause in the conversation, and Andrew held up his hands. "Sorry, ladies. I've got an appointment with an admiral. We'll have to continue this pleasant chat at a later date." He stood. "Toni, walk me to the door. We've got details to iron out."

"Sure thing." She rose as well.

Andrew made polite good-byes and they left the lounge.

"Do you really have a meeting with an admiral?"

"Why would I lie?" He grinned down at her. "I'd invite you along, but it's not related to your assignment."

"That's fine. You give me the schedule and I'll be wherever I'm supposed to. I'm in need of action."

He turned at the door, then stood back and looked at her, up and down. The confident façade faded. "Um...Toni, we're friends, aren't we...sort of?"

"Sure. Any two people who went through what we did had better be friends."

"Right. And we've had this conversation before, so I know you won't take it the wrong way."

"Take what the wrong way."

"Well...I wasn't joking when I said you were looking good. You're looking very good. Too good, if you don't mind my saying so. Chakka noticed it too."

She frowned. "Now you've really got me in space. Chakka?"

"Yeah. Pheromones. You've changed."

"I don't understand."

He took her arm. "Let's keep walking. Look, I remember you from two years ago. Never had any trouble getting along with the guys, right? Nobody ever came on to you, nobody ever bothered you, right?"

"Nobody but you."

He grinned. "That was something else, and you know it." His face became serious. "What about now? As they say, how's your love life? I don't want any details, but in general."

She waited while the heat left her face. Then she looked at him. "You're getting at something, aren't you?"

"Yeah, I think so."

"Well, then, my love life has been fine. I thought it was just the different atmosphere, you know? Not being a full-time Commando anymore, working with civilians and scientists, not having to play the role. Are you telling me it's more than that?"

"It could be. Chakka figures you've gained three kilos. You were pretty small to start with, so it makes a big difference. Tell you what. Why don't you meet me at the base hospital tomorrow at..." there was a pause while he checked his augment. "Oh nine thirty. Go to the Imaging Lab. We'll check this out properly."

He slapped her shoulder, and she could feel the strength in his hand. "Don't worry about it. You might be right. Sometimes your life changes and you change along with it."

"Right. And sometimes Freighty reaches in and flicks a switch or two."

"Yeah. Sometimes he does."

4. TEST RESULTS

Promptly at 09:30 the next morning the two of them were sitting in a sleek, modern office high in the Space Arm Medical Wing. The only indication of the medical nature of the meeting was the lab coat worn by the man behind the desk.

...who was reading his viewer and not looking at all happy. "This seems to be rather irregular, ma'am."

"In what way?" She glanced at the auguars, stretched out on either side. "Chakka and Nzinga have spent weeks in this facility."

The doctor swivelled to face them and laced his fingers together on his desktop. "The auguars are fine. It's these tests. They are not done on a whim. They are highly personal and the results can have psychological ramifications." He gestured towards the screen. "One of the subjects is a minor, and we have no parental permission."

He met her eyes and held them. "It would be wise for me to ask what is going on, here."

Toni had no answer. She glanced at Andrew.

He grinned. "Of course, Doctor. But before you give Toni the third degree, perhaps you should look at who authorized the procedures."

The doctor glanced at his screen, then looked more closely. "You. You authorized them. You're only sixteen years old. Where do you get the legal right..."

Andrew shook his head. "I had hoped to do this the easy way, Doctor, but if you insist. Will you take a look at your viewscreen again?"

Once more the doctor did a double take. "How did that get up there?"

"Read what it says."

"It's my bank account dashboard, and it authorizes a transfer of..." The man's eyebrows shot up and he stared at Andrew. "...of a thousand planetoids to you!"

"That's right. Oh, don't worry about it. It isn't a bribe, and it isn't a threat. All you have to do is void it and it will go away. It's just a demonstration of who you are dealing with."

The doctor took a moment to make sure his accounts were all in order, then closed down his terminal and faced them. "All right. At least you have demonstrated your competence. Why do you want these tests?"

"That's classified information, Dr. Proust, but all you need to know is that the two of us will be in close proximity in isolation for a considerable length of time. There have been some recent unexplained changes to Lieutenant Jacobs' physiognomy, and we want to be sure they won't cause problems."

"I see." After a brief frown, the doctor's face cleared. "Yes, that would be a good reason for the testing." He picked up a tablet and glanced at the screen as he stood. "Shall we proceed? The lab is down two floors."

From there on it was routine, with the usual poking and prodding and measuring and sampling of every fluid available. Toni couldn't help but notice that very little was done by machine. Human technicians controlled every aspect. *Nobody is taking any chances. That should be consoling...*

...then it was all over, and they were sitting back in the office of the head honcho, who looked much more content with the situation. "So. There we have it." He flicked his tablet and the results appeared on the larger viewscreen.

Toni stared at the columns. "I'm sure that's all very satisfying, sir, but it's just numbers to me. What does it mean?"

The doctor mused. "Basically, you're within parameters. Both a bit above the norm in the sexual response areas, but that's to be expected."

"It is? Why?"

The doctor grinned. "Ensign Collingwood is sixteen years old." Then his face took on a thoughtful look. "You're the interesting one."

"Being interesting is never a good sign. In what way?"

23

"Well, when the results started coming in, I took the liberty of checking your background. Are you the Toni Jacobs that took gold in judo two years running in the Humanorm Junior World Championships?" He flicked the screen. "And then bronze in wrestling in the Humanorm Olympics three years later? Yes, and then you disappeared...just about the time you enlisted. Well, that explains that. Why didn't you continue your competitive career in Space Arm?"

"I joined the Commandos."

"And..."

"Commandos don't play games, Doctor. We don't score points to win or lose. When we train with our cadre, it isn't a contest. It's a training session. You win by learning something new. There's no place for competition in a Commando squad."

The doctor had been consulting his data again. "Yes, that follows. There are very few Commandos listed in the winning statistics of the Spacer's Olympics. I don't need to wonder why."

"Now my augment keeps me out of humanorm competition of any sort, and the Pro Olympics...let's just say I'd rather stay human."

"Yes, that explains it."

"But it doesn't explain the test results."

"Why not? You're normal."

"But I never was before."

"You weren't?"

"I don't think so. There were times when I wondered if I had any gender at all. I never had relationship problems with my cadre, because I never had relationships. Not gender-related ones. I had plenty of good friends and bonded well with my fellow Commandos, but no relationships. And don't bother to ask about menstrual patterns, because I never had any. Menstruation, yes. Just no patterns."

"I see. And this situation continued until...?

"Until I left my Commando team and went to work with the Feline Augment Corps. There wasn't enough time for training, and no one of my calibre to work with. Now I hit the gym when I can, but I can't keep my weight down. I'm having having regular menstrual cycles, with the associated mood swings. That's downright scary. Plus I started attracting male attention. That part was even more scary, at least at first."

"And that's what you're worried about."

"Shouldn't I be? What's going on?"

"Delayed pubertal development."

She took that in, especially the casual attitude in the delivery. "There's a name for it?"

"Oh, yes. It's well documented. Competitive gymnastics, ballet, figure skating, that sort of comprehensive lifestyle and activity level. It's a matter of nutrition, exercise, somatotype and other factors. Once the training is released, the body sometimes goes back to its normal functions. You're lucky. By the time subjects reach your age there is usually permanent change. You seem to be merrily turning back the clock."

"So I get to go through puberty as a twenty-four-year-old. Wonderful." She regarded Andrew with a frown. "What are you smirking about?"

He wiped his hand across his mouth and held it out in a defensive gesture. "Nothing, Lieutenant. Nothing at all."

Now the doctor was smiling. "An extended period of isolation in close proximity? That ought to be interesting."

Toni calmed herself. "Do you have any advice for us?"

"Without further knowledge of your situation, I can't give you much that your mother wouldn't have told you years ago about getting along with the opposite gender. May I assume you'll be in a climate-controlled environment?"

Andrew scoffed. "Easy guess. Of course we'll be on a spaceship."

"I had surmised. Well, the first thing is to turn the scrubbers up."

"The scrubbers?"

"The air filters. You mean they don't tell you?"

25

She exchanged glances with Andrew. "Tell us what?"

The doctor grinned. "I'm sure you've been on passenger liners. You know how warm and friendly they always seem? Now think about Space Arm vessels. Businesslike, brisk, yes?"

She nodded. "I always thought that was subtle stuff like paint colour, temperature and smells."

He shook his head. "Pheromones, mostly natural. The result of large numbers of people in a closed environment. Space Arm vessels regulate the air much more carefully to select just the right molecular content. If you want a more businesslike atmosphere, adjust your scrubbers."

Andrew had that blank look that indicated he was on gestalt. It didn't take long. "The capability is there if you know where to look. *Diablo* will take care of it."

The doctor rubbed his hands together. "And at the risk of sounding like a training video, remember that you are members of the Space Arm, with the right and responsibility to uphold our tradition and reputation."

They both stood and saluted. The doctor returned the salute with a rather sloppy one of his own. "Good luck on the mission, wherever it is."

They turned to go, but Andrew hesitated. "Oh, Doctor, can I give you a word of advice?"

"I suppose so…"

"You probably thought it was more secure to do your banking from your Space Arm account. It is, but it also exposes you to a much higher grade of reprobate." He grinned. "Such as myself."

"You suggest I do my banking from my private server."

"I do. If you don't trust your bank, get a different bank." He held out his hand. "It's been an interesting morning, Dr. Proust. Thank you for the time and the information."

The doctor shook it. "It's been an interesting morning for me, as well." He shook Toni's hand. "I really meant the good luck part. I think you'll handle the rest without too much trouble. I've rarely seen a pair with their heads screwed on better."

As they left the medical centre, she glanced at Andrew. "He knows where we're going, doesn't he?"

"With his clearance, he could find out. But we've given up on keeping the Barnard System hidden. It's rather big, you know. We just follow normal security procedures and save the hocus-pocus stuff for when it's needed."

"Fair enough. After all, we're just making a personnel transfer."

"Exactly. And we have the second-fastest ship in the human sphere. I sincerely doubt if anybody cares enough about what we're doing to interfere, even if they could catch us."

She walked a few paces in silence. "So, our problems are going to come from inside the ship, not outside."

He raised a hand. "That's been solved for us as well. A message from the Diplomatic Corps caught up to me last night. I didn't want to bother you with it until this other business was sorted. We may have our chaperone."

"Good. Who is it and why is she coming? Or he."

"Her name's Morissa Goodall. Alfino sent a request for a specialist to deal with the official angle of the barwolf investigation. You and Nzinga will be working on the scientific and social interface. Paws on the ground. She'll be the expert responsible for collecting data for the legal and political assessment."

"And how does a person prepare for a job like that?"

"She's an exenocultural anthropologist."

"There really is such a thing?"

Andrew grinned. "I dug into her background. I think she pretty well created the discipline."

"Aha. Another child prodigy, pushing the boundaries of human science. You two ought to get along pretty well."

"Right. Maybe you'll end up as the chaperone."

"That would suit me just fine. When do we meet her?"

"In a couple of days. She's been teaching at the South African College of Applied Psychology and she needs time to wrap up her affairs."

"Good. This is starting to look much more like a normal assignment."

"I'd like to think so." He skipped a step and swung a hip into hers, knocking her momentarily off stride. "I'd hate to have to spend the whole trip walking on eggshells."

Even before she had regained her balance her right fist was jabbing him, not gently, in the ribs. "You got that right."

5. BACK IN SPACE

Andrew did not seem to be constrained by the bureaucratic hassles that usually hindered expedition prep. For the next week he was away on a whirlwind tour of meetings and media events, all of which fell into place with surprising ease. He didn't say much about it, and Toni didn't ask, but a few comments he dropped led her to believe that he was shameless in his use of his family name, Freighty's clout and the *Diablo* gestalt's ability to subvert pretty much any communications system when necessary.

A videoconference with Morissa Goodall revealed her to be in her late twenties, pleasant faced enough to be considered pretty in a blonde, washed-out British sort of way. And, it seemed, interested in the idea having another young woman on board.

When Toni raised the point with Andrew, he grinned. "Maybe she wants protection from me."

She shook her head. "Doomed to disappointment." Then she shot him a glare. "At least she'd better be!"

He held up his hands, laughing. "Now, don't go all Mumbot on me, Toni. You know I know better."

"I don't know any such thing. I just don't want the situation any more complicated than in already is. And I'm sorry about the Mumbot thing, but I'm your superior officer, and worse than that, I'm responsible to your mother. My choices are limited."

"And everybody's afraid of my Mum." He sighed. "Picture the rest of my life. There I'll be at fifty, an admiral in the Space Arm, and people will still be looking after me for fear I'll stub my toe and my mother will be upset."

"The gods grant that we all live that long."

"And which gods might that be?"

"I dunno. Any that care to take a hand. As long as one of them isn't named Freighty, I'll be happy. So, what's the schedule, now?"

"Morissa is coming in tomorrow from Joburg. She has to meet with somebody-or-other in the Diplomatic Corps the day after to get her final briefing and endure that useless half-hour

Otherwhere Prep lecture, and then we're free to pull the pin. Anything holding you back?"

She grinned. "Tearful farewell scenes with ardent admirers of the opposite gender, I suppose."

"From what I hear those need to be short and sweet or they become long and complicated."

"I'll do my best to heed your experienced advice."

"Good." He stood and nudged Chakka with his toe. "We'll be diplomatic and give Morissa the option of an extra day, but in lieu of anything else, we blast off in two days."

"Good enough." She ruffled Nzinga's neck. "Hear that, kid? You're headed for space."

Emotion: wild enthusiasm.

Emotion: resigned boredom.

Andrew laughed. "Don't worry, Chakka, I'm sure there will be lots to keep you occupied."

Toni wrinkled her forehead. "Be careful what you ask for."

"Oh. Yeah."

* * *

In person, Morissa Goodall was as pale and pleasant as expected, but taller. Looking at her two crewmates, Toni decided they would make a nice couple. If she wasn't twenty-eight years old.

And if Morissa didn't treat Andrew like…well, like she treated the auguars. Acknowledged for the sake of good manners, and then ignored until needed.

Being the centre of someone's attention was rather embarrassing, but Toni assumed a role as senior officer and took the lead on the discussion. Andrew, chuckling quietly through their augments, faded away to prepare the ship for launch.

Morissa sat on the skimpy couch in the tiny mess hall/lounge and looked around. "I've put up with a whole lot worse in bush camp." She smiled. "At least I can hope the shower water will be hot."

Toni answered the smile. "Excess heat is a problem in Otherwhere, so yes, the water's always hot and the coffee's hotter."

"Oh, I'm a tea drinker." A tiny frown wrinkled the smooth brow. "That won't be a problem, will it?"

"If you have anything exotic, make sure you tell Andrew and he'll order it."

"But I thought we were leaving tomorrow."

Toni grinned. "It takes a while to get used to having Andrew on logistics. Doors open for him. Often in the literal sense."

The woman made a moue of distaste. "I know the type."

Toni frowned. "No, I don't think you do. That's not what I'm talking about. He gets things done. How do you think we managed to get you out of your position and ready for space in six days?"

"With a whole lot of influence. Doors opened in front of me and closed very firmly behind me the moment I made my decision."

"Well, that's Andrew."

"Yes, that's money." Again the smooth brow furrowed in disproval.

Toni shook her head. "If you're thinking of the Collingwood connection, forget it. They're small potatoes compared to the circles you're moving in now."

She sat in the only other lounge chair, as slim as the couch, with a stretchy fabric that felt comfortable at several G levels. "What do you know about Factory 4-80?"

The other shrugged. "Pretty much what everyone does, I guess. An alien factory thousands of years old, headed for Earth to bring us a New Industrial Revolution. With all its corresponding problems, no doubt."

"That's not a bad analysis, except that Freighty is very aware of the problems he could cause for the human race and determined not to let it happen."

"Freighty?"

"That's what Andrew named the factory when he was five years old. It's a long story, and it's Andrew's to tell. For the moment, just be happy that Andrew and his mother are watching out for humanity's best interests, and Freighty listens to them above everyone else. And that goes double for your barwolves."

"In what way?"

"We'll have time for a whole lot of briefing once we get into space, but the basic problem, as people in your position have been battling for centuries, is that once commercial interests figure out how to make money off the Tree Planet, and more specifically if they can make money off the barwolves themselves, there is going to be incredible pressure to downgrade the barwolf society and loosen the quarantine. Arborea, as they're now calling it, is the only other planet in the Human sphere where we could actually live without tech aid, so it's a real flash point. I don't envy you your job, but the *Nighthawk* gestalt will be your best ally."

"Space Arm is my best friend, is it?"

"No, Natalia and I are only the Space Arm part of it. Andrew is the turning point. He's Space Arm but he's also Freighty...you know, Freighty might be useful to you as well."

"Why should he care?"

"Test case. He's in the same position you are. A superior intellect judging a backward species to decide how much help to give them so that they make progress without destroying themselves. Yes, you really need to talk to Freighty."

"I'll take that into consideration. I have no intention of leaving any stone unturned. I am aware of the gravity of my responsibility, and I am determined to make the absolute best choices for my clients."

Toni reached across and slapped the other woman on the shoulder. "Atta girl. You go into the situation with that attitude, we might all come out the other end in one piece."

She stood, grinning, trying to ignore the conflicting emotions that ran across Morissa's face.

Crap on a plate. Is this going to be a problem?

What problem?

Don't worry about it, Andrew. Let's get this bird ready to fly.

Twelve hours, give or take. We're not advertising.

Your call. Pumpkin and I are ready.

Yeah, she's ready. She's already shoved Chakka out of his accel couch on the bridge. He looks rather silly in her couch. He hangs over.

I'll have a word.

No, she can have it all she wants until blast-off. I know how to pick my battles.

Good thought.

* * *

Ten hours later Andrew came on the ship's com. "Crew prepare for liftoff in ten minutes."

Toni glanced over at her new shipmate. "There are only two accel couches on the bridge. The rest of the crew uses their bunks."

"All right."

"Do you need a hand figuring out the straps?"

"I don't think so. I checked them out already."

"If you have a problem, just say so out loud. *Diablo* will help you solve it or route it to me through the ship's com."

"I'll go strap in now, just in case."

"Roger." She grinned. "Well, this is it. We're off."

"Are there any traditions?"

Toni lifted a fist. "Smooth ride."

The other bumped her fist awkwardly. "Smooth ride sounds like a good idea."

Toni turned back in the doorway. "*Diablo* is one of the smoothest ships I've ridden in. Except for the huge acceleration, you'll never notice."

Morissa smiled. "I'll take that as a promise."

Toni entered the bridge, interested in the seating arrangements. Sure enough, Nzinga was still stretched out on the large circular pad in the very bow, Chakka perched on the smaller one to starboard. She raised her eyebrows to Andrew.

He nodded. "Okay, cats. Into your proper spots. Blastoff in three."

With a great show of casual boredom, the smaller auguar rose from her position, stretched, and strolled over to stare at Chakka. He seemed to be asleep.

Toni and Andrew shared a grin and went on with their own prep.

Nzinga reached out with a hesitant paw and patted the larger cat's ear.

He raised his head, yawned, then stood up and stretched. Only then did he get off the bed, towering over his smaller companion. He regarded her a moment, then leaned down and licked the side of her face with a big, long slurp before strolling over to his own couch and lying down. The automatic restraints folded over him, and he wriggled himself comfortable.

Nzinga watched him, then circled her own bed, approaching it from the opposite direction. She sniffed around, and when she was satisfied that all was in order, she lay down. When the restraints reached out, she pushed against them in several directions as if to tell them where she wanted them.

Finally, she lay still.

"Any idea what was going on there?"

"Not really. Somebody got something straight."

Andrew grinned. "I have a feeling we're going to be well entertained on this trip."

Diablo, give us the count out loud, please. We have guests aboard.

"We have clearance to depart. Liftoff in thirty seconds...

...in twenty seconds...

...in ten seconds...five...three, two, one. Smooth ride, folks."

A great surge of power pushed against their backs, and the clouds overhead rushed towards them. Soon they broke free into bright sunshine and a blue sky fading slowly to black as the little ship gained velocity and altitude.

"How are you doing back there, Morissa?"

"Fine. That was smoother than any commercial flight I ever had. I love these big viewscreens."

"It helps that we got so quickly through the part of the atmosphere dense enough to cause turbulence. In about thirty seconds we'll be in vacuum. Rendezvous with our fuel tank in ten minutes, and we'll be floating for about fifteen while we connect up. Have you been weightless before?"

"No, I haven't."

"Well, enjoy yourself. Flap around all you like, if your stomach can handle it. I'll give you plenty of warning before we hit gravity again."

"Great."

Toni was unfastening her straps. "I'll wander back and be nearby. You never can tell." She strolled along the companionway to the lounge to take one last scout around for objects that might float loose. Soon the roar of the engines died and gravity disappeared. She relaxed in mid-air, floating across to chase down a pen that had worked its way out from under the couch.

You could have left the internal gravity plates on.

I could have, but it interferes with maneuvering when we're in a gravity field even as weak as Earth's is out here. Think of a spinning bicycle wheel. You try to nudge it out of line and it resists.

35

The inertial fields have inertia? Whoda thunk?

Plus, I wanted to give our passenger a taste of fun. We don't do much free floating in this bird. Too busy accelerating.

Hence the fuel tank.

Right. Which at the moment...is...

A "thunk" shuddered through the spaceframe.

...attached. It takes a bit for the electronics to boot up and do their checks, and then we'll be away.

I'll check on our passenger.

Toni swam over and tapped on Morissa's door. "Everything all right?"

"Just a minute."

Something thumped against the door, and then it opened slightly. Morissa pulled it further, then figured out how to put one hand on the frame and the other on the door to settle herself.

"Well done. Hinged doors are a real problem in weightlessness."

The other woman smiled. "I figured that out the moment I released the latch and it started swinging."

"How's it going?"

"Pretty well, I think."

"Ready for the wide-open spaces?"

"Maybe."

"Just launch yourself very lightly for another object like the table. The chairs are clamped, too." She grinned. "Just try not to leave fingerprints on the viewscreens. It irritates the experienced hands."

"I'll do my best. I've done a lot of swimming. Shouldn't that help?"

"It should, but the only way to find out..." she gestured towards the room.

"Here I go."

Morissa pushed out into the room, floating gently past the table, which she tapped lightly to redirect herself to the wall.

There, she hit harder than she expected and bounced off, flailing a bit until she reached the ceiling, where she cushioned herself gently with her fingertips and came to rest. Smiling, she turned and pushed off, performing a creditable front roll before she hit the far wall, again coming to a dead stop.

"Hey, that looked pretty good."

"Diving. It's like riding a bicycle, I guess."

"Ahem. Sorry to spoil your fun, ladies, but we're ready to hit the outer limits of the galaxy. Well, we have enough fuel to go about eight lights. Ten, if you have a few years to get there."

Tony grinned at her companion and spoke aloud and in her augment. *"Let's take the shorter route. We have business to attend to. Give us a minute to find the floor."*

"Let me know."

The two women pushed off and anchored themselves to chairs. *"Ready to roll, Captain."*

Diablo's voice came over the com.

"Easy accel in five...three, two, one, on. Slow increase to one point five G."

Andrew's voice came on. "Watch your balance. We'll be running a G and a half for the next hour or so, just to confuse anyone who might be watching. After that we settle down to a normal G and we're home free. In three and a half months."

"Thanks, Andrew. We're fine here for the moment."

Morissa frowned. "Wait a minute. This gravity is downwards." She pointed forward, towards the bridge. "We're going that way. Shouldn't the gravity be...?" she pointed aft, over her shoulder.

"That's right. On most ships it would be. In *NightHawk's* habitation ring the furniture all shifts and the back wall becomes the floor."

"That's what I thought."

"The ship you're riding in right now is pure science fiction. The system controls the inertial resistance caused by acceleration and merely deflects it ninety degrees, using 64% less power than it would need to null the original force and create a new one. Freighty may not give Humanity the technology for these inertial systems for a decade or more."

"Why not?"

Toni moved to the couch, which was marginally more comfortable. "When you're dealing with any intelligent species, I bet you have all sorts of rules about interfering with their culture. Chimpanzees and dolphins and the like, right?"

"Certainly."

"Well, I don't think I'm speaking out of turn when I tell you that Freighty has had experience with several different spacefaring species, including the people who created him. None of those events turned out well."

"I see. He's worried that humanity isn't ready for some of his technology. Of course." She sat straighter. "I'm beginning to see his problems."

"Right. Now, he's an ArIn, so apply Asimov's Laws of Robotics."

"You mean Factory 4-80..."

"I'm not sure of the details. You'll have to ask Andrew about it. But Freighty has programmed constraints, and he was forced to make up a new one after the *Clyde* battle: no weapons. And more recently he has broadened that to include anything that could be made into a weapon."

"And better inertial dampening means better fighting ships."

"Exactly. Humanity is doing just fine with the gravity systems we have. With the more powerful engines Freighty is helping us design, we're making great progress. But good intertial systems make better warships because better crew protection means increased maneuverablity. So, he's limiting our development. Nobody should be in a hurry."

"I'll have to speak with this Freighty being. I'm beginning to get interested in his thought processes."

"You can speak to him any time."

"What?"

Toni grinned. "Sort of. I'm warning you, it won't be like anything you expect."

Morissa sat straighter. "Of course it won't. That's what I'm here for."

Toni made a quick augment connection to receive an okay from Andrew, then took a deep breath.

"Here goes. Freighty? Are you there? I've got someone I'd like you to meet."

To her surprise, the figure that appeared on the viewscreen was Freighty in his formal "South European Businessman" guise.

"Good afternoon, Lieutenant."

"Um...hi, Freighty. You need to meet our new crewmember."

The avatar turned his head. "Ah, yes. The soon-to-be-illustrious descendent of the illustrious original social anthropologist. I've been waiting to meet you."

Morissa glanced to Toni, then back to the avatar. "Pleased to meet you...?"

"All my friends call me Freighty. Please."

"Freighty. Yes. I've been hearing about you."

He grinned. "Oh, don't take everything Toni says at face value. Her head has been turned by my sparkling personality."

"Freighty, will you excuse us a minute? Please shut yourself down and don't come back until I ask you."

The avatar frowned, then cleared his brow and smiled graciously. "Of course, Lieutenant. Whatever you say."

"Diablo?"

"Yes, Lieutenant?"

"Will you please make sure the mouse is in his box and can't get out?"

"Certainly, Lieutenant. I will commence the security protocols."

"Thank you."

She turned to her puzzled companion. "I obviously didn't prepare you enough. Freighty is always playing games at several different levels. The games are meant to lull us into a false sense of security. When we discover the game, that just makes our feeling stronger and falser, because we think we have outsmarted him. We haven't."

"But how could that," Morissa flicked a hand toward the screen, "have been a game? He seemed perfectly normal."

Toni made a wry grin. "That should be your first clue. Nothing about him is normal. That is not his usual avatar. It's an image he uses when he wants to impress people with his suave human qualities. It's as fake as his usual avatar."

"Which is...?"

"Let's try again. Freighty, will you appear in your usual form, please? *Diablo*, let him out of his cage."

The viewscreen flickered, and the mouse appeared in prison garb, a huge ball attached by chain to his ankle. "Toni, you're always spoiling my fun."

"Sorry about that, but this is too serious a situation for games."

He shrugged and appeared in his usual blue shorts and lime-green shoes. "No problem. It used too much memory anyway." He turned to Morissa. "Pleased to meet you in any case. I gather you and I find ourselves in similar circumstances, only at different levels."

"Ah...yes, we were just observing that."

Micha smiled. "And how do you think your great-great-whatever-great aunt would have handled it?"

"How do you know about my relationship to Jane Goodall?"

"You mean Jane *Morris* Goodall? I'm sure Toni will be pleased to inform you that I have an encyclopedic knowledge of human history and culture. As you may gather, I am only an avatar with a small portion of my full memory stored with *Diablo*, but when we reach closer to re-ti communication with the factory, I'm sure I will be able to direct you to some appropriate literature. That is, if you don't know about it already. You have a strong academic background already. I was particularly impressed with your treatise on the intelligence of termite communities."

"You were?"

"Morissa, he's playing games again. He can be a great deal of use to you, exactly in the way he has indicated, but never assume you know why he's doing it."

"Toni, if I had feelings, I assure you they would be gravely injured right about now."

"Then it's a good thing you don't have any, because I want to make this very clear to you. Morissa is going into a very difficult situation, and the fate of a species rests in her hands. You could be of great use to her. Likewise, she could be of use to you, because she is one of the few humans who has studied the situation you find yourself in. That potential relationship is too important to be spoiled by your manipulation, which, in case you haven't noticed, gives humans a very cynical reaction to you."

"Ah. You put it so clearly. Prime. I will follow your instructions. I will treat Miss Goodall with all the respect due a fellow academic in a subject related to my own. Does that make you happy?"

Toni turned to Morissa. "And that's a game, too, but it's the best one you're going to get." She refocused her gaze on the viewscreen. "Now, Morissa and I have things to talk about. You have three months or more to chat, so will you put yourself back in your box?"

"Sure thing, Toni. Talk to you later, Morissa."

"Um...yes, Freighty. We have things to talk about."

Toni spoke aloud to keep the other woman informed. "Andrew?"

"Yes?"

"Can you ask *Diablo* to put a tracer on that avatar so we know when he's wandering around?"

"Good idea. I caught some of that. You were a little steamed."

"Sorry. I didn't know I was leaking."

"You been doing your augment isolation exercises?"

"For months. It's a slow process, though."

"Fair enough. I'm almost finished here. I'll come down for a chat."

"Great."

She turned to Morissa. "Well, there you have it. Any time you want to talk to Freighty, just call him and he'll come."

"I notice you talk to the ship the same way."

"Yes. That's a good point. We'll get Andrew to give you a security clearance so you can talk to *Diablo* as well."

"Thank you." The other woman regarded her. "You don't like Freighty much, do you?"

"Huh? No, no. I have a pretty close relationship with him, actually. Some day he's going to be my employer."

"How does that work?"

"All the original crew of the *NightHawk* are under contract to Freighty. The moment they leave the Space Arm they step into executive positions with the Factory 4-80 Fabrication Consortium."

"Then why are you so rude to him?"

Toni shrugged. "Have you ever met a person who just doesn't seem to get it? Who automatically assumes that if you talk calmly and agreeably, it means he can do anything he likes?"

Morissa' face went red. "Oh. Oh, yes. Most certainly."

"And the only way to get him to take you seriously is to stand up to him and tell him how it is? I can see from your reaction that you have. And it isn't always a "him" either. That's Freighty. The only way you can stop his manipulative games is to put your foot down."

"I see."

Toni gave a twisted grin. "And even then, don't believe you've got to the bottom of the pile. He's probably got three or four other levels going at the same time."

She leaned forward earnestly. "Morissa, we're dealing with an entity who has the power and knowledge to destroy humanity. We humans have to stand up for ourselves. We have to keep from treating him as anything but what he is: a super-intelligent and knowledgeable ArIn. We can't attribute human feelings or human motivation to him, even if he looks like a cartoon mouse.

If you run into problems with him, ask Andrew or, if possible, ask Captain O'Rourke. She's the only one who seems to know what's going on in that superbrain."

"You're telling me there is no bottom line. There's nothing about him we can count on."

"Captain O'Rourke uses one touchstone. According to her, he is duty bound by whatever rules control him to do the best he can for the human race. So, if you can persuade him that what you are doing is for the good of humanity, then suddenly you have the whole weight of his organization and the wealth of his knowledge behind you. I think you could find yourself in that position."

"But I have to remind myself that if Freighty thinks the human race will be best served if I get eaten by the barwolves..."

"I think you have the idea."

Morissa dropped her arms on the table to cushion her head.

The extra gravity must be getting to her.

Then she straightened and looked directly at Toni. "I haven't been on this ship a full day yet, and already I'm beginning to realize what I have to deal with."

She dropped her head on her arms again and didn't move for a long time.

6.TROUBLE IN THE TREES

The following morning things looked better. Morissa watched Toni muscling the exercise apparatus back into the wall, then came over to help. "If this is such an advanced ship, why do we have to do so much by manual labour?"

Toni concealed her pleasure at this change of attitude and answered casually. "Several reasons. *Diablo* started life as a stripped-out racing design, and weight continues to be important. Also, this is exercise equipment. That ought to be a hint."

The other woman smiled. "We need the exercise."

Toni glanced at her sideways. "Which reminds me to ask..."

"No, I haven't. I've been too caught up in my troubles to feel like it." She sighed and started to pull the equipment down again. "Don't help me. I need the exercise."

"Toni," Andrew's voice came over the com.

"Aye." They could have used their augments, but had decided to keep the communication as oral as possible in deference to their passenger.

"Otherwhere message coming in."

"On my way."

When she got to the bridge, the young captain was in his accel couch, staring at the forward viewscreen. She slipped into the left-hand seat. "What have we got?"

"Just downloading now. Handshake from Ambassador Pretoro, five days ago."

"That's faster than usual, isn't it?"

"Routed through Freighty's Pony Express. He doesn't use that unless he has to."

Before she could respond, the screen fizzled and cleared. Alfino sat in his office on the *Unicorn*, now the Planetary Community Embassy Station.

"Hello, Andrew, Toni, and I hope Dr. Goodall."

"Freeze, *Diablo*." He opened the ship's com. "Morissa, are you near a viewscreen?"

"I'm in the mess."

"This is for you, too."

"Thanks. I'm on it. Any excuse to stop this torture."

Toni winked at Andrew. "The viewscreen is set up so you can exercise and watch."

"Thank you, Doctor Misery."

"*Diablo*, continue."

"...Dr. Goodall. We have had progress on the Tree Planet, or should I say a notable lack of progress, but it has given us new information that I hope will help you formulate your plan of attack. And I don't use that word lightly."

His brows drew down. "Our advance party was doing well. That uninhabited island was a great place to set up the permanent camp. Only small animals, no colonies to disturb once we got away from the nesting avians on the shoreline. You can't really call them birds, but they do fly somehow.

"Once the buildings were up and the generators running, we started our population surveys. We were using our two quietest shuttles, cruising at maximum altitude, doing everything we could to stay out of notice. And it all seemed to be working.

"And then a shuttle went down. Nothing serious, just mechanical problems that made it unsafe to try to get back to base. They had time to pick a spot halfway between two packs of barwolves. One observation we have made is that the packs stay away from each other. Solo animals may travel, but the packs are restricted in their movement. We thought the crew would be safe. They set down and waited for the mechanics to come.

"It didn't work. The other shuttle had moved over to monitor the situation, and they noticed both packs drifting towards the landing site. Then they noticed four other packs filtering over their traditional boundaries, all headed in the same direction.

"Fortunately, the second shuttle pilot was a bright lad. He called an emergency abort and went in for pickup. Good thing he did. By the time he got there, the barwolves had surrounded the

45

shuttle and were in the process of destroying it. Those jaws of theirs are incredibly strong, and they were chewing through anything that wasn't space-grade hullmetal.

"The rescue shuttle swooped in, dropped a grapple and lifted the other shuttle out. They had to come back to base at low altitude because the barwolves had already compromised the air seals around the windows and entry port.

"But that wasn't the worst of it. The next day the shuttle did a flyover of the site to assess impact."

Pretoro shook his head and swallowed. "The images are appended, if you have the stomach to watch them. It was like a battleground in the old days. Torn bodies all over the place. Blood in pools in some spots. And it was spread out like a bomb blast, a couple of hundred metres in diameter, with fewer and fewer bodies at the circumference, and five or six scattered farther out. And there wasn't a barwolf in sight. It looks like the two original packs were completely wiped out, and most of the four in the immediate vicinity. The packs outside that radius were grouped as normal, functioning as if nothing had happened.

"That's our news. I'm sure you will have questions, so fire them back. I could make all sorts of suppositions, but it's not my field, and for once I'm quite happy to leave it to the experts."

He shrugged, his hands up helplessly. "Sorry to be the bearer of bad news. We're continuing the surveys, but it's going to be slower because the shuttles have to work together for safety. We were lucky to get our people out alive.

"That's all for now. I've appended the data from the surveys. Safe travels."

The screen blanked, then faded up with a horrific display of bodies torn and dismembered, with trails of reddish-brown blood running through the vegetation.

With a gesture, Andrew closed the screen down.

Miss Goodall is in distress, sir.

Toni hit the deck plates running. When she got to the mess, Morissa sprawled across the table in tears, her face buried in her arms, sobbing loudly.

Unsure what to do, Toni laid a hand on her shoulder. "We're sorry. You didn't have to see that."

Andrew, what the hell do I do?

I don't know. Give her a hug?

You get down here.

On my way.

She sat beside Morissa, put an arm across her shoulders and held her in a light squeeze until her sobs faded. When the woman seemed to be gaining control, Toni gradually released her and sat up. "Better now?"

A blotched, tear-stained face peered up at her. "That was just...so...terrible! Why would they do that? I do...don't understand!" This last part ended in a wail, and she launched herself into Toni's arms, almost knocking her over, sobbing into Toni's shoulder as if her world had ended.

Regarding Andrew helplessly, the commando held her shipmate until the sobbing stopped, then gently set her upright. "It's all right now. You won't have to look at them again."

Morissa was on the verge of breaking again. "Yes, I will. It's part of my job. The evidence has to be analyzed like a crime scene. There might be key information left behind. I know it will give me nightmares for years, but it's too late now. I have to do it."

"Well, we'll help you all we can. At least, I will. I've got more experience with this sort of thing, although I have to say, nothing like this. But let's put it all aside for the moment."

Andrew scratched his cheek with one finger. "My only question is who was in that shuttle. Spacers with augments, perhaps? That's the only explanation that makes any sense."

"Then why didn't we get attacked when we landed the first time we contacted them?

"The only difference was that we landed in one pack's territory."

"And we had Chakka with us."

"No idea which one of those was the key that set them off."

Morissa nodded. "We have two questions to answer, because there were two parts to the event."

Andrew nodded. "First half, why did the barwolves all approach the downed shuttle and attack it?"

Toni glanced again at the carnage on the viewscreen. "And once the shuttle was gone, what turned them against each other? Morissa, have you ever heard of anything like this?"

The older woman shrugged. "Apart from a human battlefield, no."

"Other pack animals?"

"When North American wolf packs have territorial battles, it's usually only the alpha males, maybe a few others. Nothing like this. Sharks have feeding frenzies, but it's not territorial. Sorry. I'm already regretting my separation from my research sources."

Andrew held up empty hands. "*Diablo* searched her database and came up blank. We'll have to ask Freighty if he has any information."

* * *

It was a gruesome job, so they decided to get it over with right away. They started working together, but soon found that Morissa was repelled by Toni's casual ability to discuss the details of the fighting, and eventually the anthropologist worked by herself. Toni was unable to influence this situation, but she made sure she worked with Andrew and monitored his reactions. He made no comments on the nature of the task, restricting his talk to analysis of the data.

Toni's worst day was when they came upon the smaller bodies. A group of cubs had been set upon and torn apart to the point where it was impossible to be sure how many there had been. Toni took care of that part of the analysis by herself and spent several hours curled up with Nzinga afterwards, stroking her auguar's fur and murmuring, her augment closed to the cub.

By mutual consent, they decided to limit their exposure to two hours a day. Toni made an effort to find light-hearted activities for the remaining time, but Morissa seemed a solitary person, preferring to close herself up in her cabin with her research and whatever else she did to occupy her private time. Andrew spent many hours in simulator mode with *Diablo,* and sometimes Toni joined him, learning the basics of piloting.

Andrew joked about it one day. "It's probably a good thing if you pick up a bit of this. You are the designated alternate pilot, you know."

"I am?"

He looked around the bridge. "Do you see anyone else?" He frowned. "Although there's a good chance that Chakka could pilot the ship. His coordination and sense of balance are far better than ours. I'm going to have to try that."

"I hope only in the simulator. I can just see us zooming all over space while he figures out how to navigate."

Andrew giggled. "Sounds like fun, but no, the pilot only needs to give *Diablo* the command decisions. She pretty well flies herself."

"Then she must be subject to Asimov's Laws, too, so she can make command decisions that affect the safety of the crew."

"Give the lady a kewpie doll."

Two weeks later, Morissa called the team together. "I think we've got everything we can out of this data, at least on a preliminary basis. There is a danger with having a small sample of information and too much time to dwell on it. It biases your mind against newer input at a later date."

Toni nodded. "Sounds reasonable."

"Let's do a recap, and maybe we can put this business out of our minds for a while."

"I can't help but agree. We need closure, even temporarily."

"Our analysis comes up with several points. First, the original site of the shuttle was the centre of the battle, but there was no concentration of bodies there. The only conclusion we can draw is that the animals that were attacking the shuttle were attacked from outside after the shuttle left. There is a definite circle of bodies about twenty-five metres in diameter. Paths of blood leading away from that area would seem to indicate fleeing victims being pulled down. Then, about fifty metres and more away, scattered small battle sites, with two or three victims. Bodies were discovered as far as half a kilometre away, some in more complete condition, suggesting perhaps they died from blood loss." She referred to her tablet.

"In all there were approximately seventy beings killed. Counts of the area done before the shuttle descended would indicate that the two packs originally involved had about fifteen members each. That would leave ten members killed from each of the surrounding packs, and that doesn't add up. If a large number of animals attacked a smaller group, we would not expect equal losses from both sides. We can't be certain, but it seems probable that packs turned on other packs, and we can't ignore the possibility that pack members turned on each other. The damage done to the bodies leads us in that direction. I don't want to go into too much detail, but these animals have heavy, segmented armour. The only way to kill one is to literally tear a piece of the armour off and damage the body inside. That, plus the nature of the creatures' teeth, is what causes the excessive destruction and gore."

"Perhaps a frenzy of some sort."

"It can't be counted out." Morissa's face paled, and she swallowed deeply several times.

Andrew gave her a moment to regain her poise before he asked, "I suppose there's nothing to suggest that behaviour like this is any function of intelligence, or lack of it?"

She grimaced. "Have you ever seen images of a World War One battlefield?"

"Point taken. This is just another set of data to help you make your analysis. It doesn't change your job, just makes it harder."

"It will, if every time we set down we cause a massacre."

Toni shook her head. "But the first contact Andrew and I had with them was the opposite. You've seen the video and the reproductions of Andrew's augment images."

"That's what I don't understand. They exhibited intelligence and complex social behaviours, pretty much within the realm of similar Earth species."

Andrew pressed his lips together. "Well, I guess that's what happens when you start dealing with aliens. They do alien things."

Morissa nodded. "Expecting similarities to Earth species to predict the actions of aliens would be a large mistake. That's the lesson my famous ancestor taught the so-called scientists of her time. They viewed all animals from the human viewpoint and assumed that actions that looked human were identical to human. Thus, actions that did not look human did not show intelligence."

Toni sighed. "Applying your battlefield analogy, none of this data changes anything. Can we put it behind us and try to resume a normal life?"

Morissa looked around the cramped space. "As normal a life as we can manage."

"Right. But I think we ought to ship the images off to Freighty for his comments."

"I need all the help I can get, and an alien viewpoint might be what we want."

Toni slapped the table. "Right. I'll take care of that. And I think we ought to have something special for supper tonight. Might I suggest vegetarian?"

Toni wasn't looking forward to Otherwhere, but at least it would be a change from poring over images of blood and mayhem. However, she was beginning to worry about Morissa's attitude, so she pulled Andrew aside the day before they reached Light Transfer Velocity.

He waved her concerns away. "She's had the usual prep class. What more can we do? Until you experience it re-ti, nothing can prepare you for Otherwhere. I've talked to her about it, and she seems to have it figured out pretty well."

"Yeah, like she had her work with the barwolves figured out. She's an academic, Andrew, from a protected environment. I don't see any evidence that she's ever been subject to the kind of mental stress she's already under. And nobody finds Otherwhere like they expected. I certainly didn't."

"You're right, but I've done what I can. One thing I learned from the captain about leadership is you can't do it for them."

"True. It's not my place to interfere, that's for sure. We'll just have to monitor her closely. What else can we do?"

He gave a faint shadow of his usual grin. "I had to stop my last passengers from attacking each other with table forks. We've got this one outnumbered. We should do fine."

"That's the attitude." She raised her voice a touch. "How long till LTV, *Diablo*?"

"Seventeen hours, thirteen minutes, ma'am. Give or take a second or two.

"Thanks, *Diablo,* minutes are close enough."

"I thought so. Humans are rather imprecise at times. Have you noticed this, Lieutenant?"

She rolled her eyes at Andrew. "We don't have the computing power you have, so we round data to reasonable decimal points. Thank you for the input, *Diablo*."

"My pleasure, ma'am."

Andrew turned to her. "Remember, we have a bunch of research to do while we're out there."

"The Collingwood Otherwhere Augment Communication Theory. How could I forget? I'm the second-string guinea pig."

"Don't be snooty. Us academics won't stand for it. I did a bunch of tests on myself during the inbound trip, but most of the communication stuff requires two people with organics." He grinned. "Which was the real reason I rushed to volunteer for taxi duty. I hope that doesn't make you feel slighted as a person."

"If I really thought it was true, I promise you I would make a valiant attempt to feel upset. What are your research methods?"

He shrugged. "Pretty boring, actually. Data collecting. Measurements and scans of brain activity under usage and at rest. Freighty has created some instrumentation, but this is new stuff to him as well, so I'm not sure how much help it will be."

"As long as it doesn't feed back and fry my augments, I suppose that's all right."

"I guess that's a possibility, but Freighty doesn't like to waste valuable resources, so I think we're pretty much okay in that respect."

"Dynamite. Can't wait."

"Don't worry. I want to make some baseline tests this afternoon, and we can start the real stuff as soon as we transit tomorrow. We only have about 4 weeks in Otherwhere, so we have to get at it if we're going to see any change over time."

* * *

They kept a close eye on their passenger for the first week of Otherwhere, but she seemed to be handling it. One day when the two of them were on the bridge and Morissa was in her cabin, Toni checked in with Andrew.

"How do you think she's doing?"

"Hard to tell. She's basically a solitary person already."

"She's very self-contained."

53

"Well, she got a real kick in the butt from those pictures. As she said herself, she had no idea what problems she would have to face. Now she's got some problems to dig her teeth into, and I guess she's gnawing away."

Toni shook her head. "I don't like that image."

"Ah. Any point in asking her how she's managing?"

"I don't want to overdo it. I check with her at least once a day. I'm playing the 'concerned senior officer' role, which is where she seems to have slotted me."

"And…"

"She always shrugs and says she's doing all right, considering."

He shook his head. "Well, let me know if you see any change."

"Certainly." She grinned at him. "On that topic, how are we doing?"

"What? You and me? I think all that hoopla just before we left was a big red herring."

She frowned. "Dr. Proust didn't think so, and he spent a good deal of his precious time and resources making sure everything was all right."

"And it is." He glanced at her. "Don't you think so?"

She wavered a hand back and forth, palm down. "So-so. Nothing different from any other time."

"Good. I won't let my guard down, though."

She stared at him. "You have your guard up?"

"Don't you?"

"Now that you mention it, I sort of do. Matter of habit."

"Great. I'm developing the habit. With a little help from *Diablo's* air scrubbers, we'll be fine."

"That's one problem that wasn't, anyway."

He shook his head. "Did you ever notice how that happens all the time? You work so hard to predict what's going to go down and prepare for it, and then something else comes at you from behind a comet."

"Yep. That's life in the Commandos."

"And in the Space Arm."

"And in the rest of the universe, I guess. We'll handle it."

"Considering the alternative, I guess we'd better."

She punched his arm. "That's a very mature attitude, lad. You keep it up and we'll make an officer of you some day."

* * *

The final straw didn't come completely out of the blue, and later Toni kicked herself for not seeing it coming. The three of them were sitting around the mess table after lunch one day. Morissa was reading something on a tablet, Toni had her handgun laid out in pieces and was examining it for wear as she did once a week, even if it hadn't been fired. Andrew was staring off into space, which meant that he was probably working through some incomprehensible problem with *Diablo*. He caught her glance, raised an eyebrow and went back to his focus. She smiled to herself. Nothing complicated; simple human contact made Otherwhere bearable.

"You're talking about me, aren't you?"

Andrew's eyes focused. "What?"

"On your augments. I saw that look. You're talking about me in your augments."

His glance shot to Toni, who shrugged.

"See? You're doing it again. You just said something like, 'Here she goes again,' and Toni just answered, 'What can you do with a person like that?' At least neither of you laughed this time."

Again, the wordless appeal from Andrew.

Toni reached out and touched Morissa's arm to get her attention. "We said nothing of the sort. Since you just spoke, neither of us has used an augment. What you saw was exactly the communication we made, and, considering what a shock your accusation was, I think a small response was forgivable."

"It might be a small response, but when it's happening day after day, all day, it begins to wear, you know? Now I know what a deaf person feels like. All that communication going on around you, and you think maybe you know what it means, but you could have it completely backwards."

"I'm glad you said that, Morissa, because you do have it wrong. Yes, Andrew and I are concerned for your welfare, but you seem to be doing all right, and you haven't said anything, so what were we to do? What's the problem?"

The woman dropped her face into her hands. "I'm just so lonely. I feel like I'm the only human in a million miles." She raised tearstained features. "I don't think I can handle two more months of this. But what else can I do?" She dropped her head again.

Toni and Andrew stared at each other over her bowed head.

She needs a hug.

Andrew shrugged helplessly. *Not from me!*

Yes. From you.

What if she takes it the wrong way?

She won't. Believe me.

He frowned at her. *Do you know something I don't?*

Yes. Give her a hug.

He knelt by her chair and laid an arm around the woman's shoulders, coaxing her head against his chest. "We didn't know, Morissa. We thought you were just that sort of a person, you know. Solitary. We thought you wanted your privacy."

She snuffled and mumbled into his shirt. "But I am. At first I liked it. I thought I'd be fine. But I'm not. I'm just sooo alooone!" The last was a wail, and she threw her arms around him, sobbing.

After a while her breathing calmed.

Andrew relaxed his arm. "Um...Morissa?"

"Yes?" The sound was still muffled against his chest.

"My knees are killing me."

"Oh!" She jolted upright. "I'm sorry. I didn't know..." She looked about to break into tears again.

"No, no, it's all right. I don't mind. They're just stiff. Can I stand up, now?"

"Of course. I'm fine. No, I'm really fine. But I'm so sorry. That was unforgivable of me." She dabbed at her face with a damp hand, straightening her shoulders. "So unprofessional."

Toni knelt beside her. "Morissa, there's no such thing as professional when Otherwhere starts to get to you."

"Otherwhere?"

"Yes, we told you, remember? Otherwhere makes everybody react like that."

"But not you. You've both been as cheerful as ever. And the worse I got, the more cheerful you got, and I thought it must be only me."

Toni sighed. "And we were trying to cheer you up." She , too, rose from her knees and went back to her chair. "You obviously need to talk more about this."

Morissa wiped a sleeve across her cheek. "I obviously don't know what I thought I knew."

"Right. So, go and clean yourself up, wash your face in cold water and come back and sit down. I'll give you lesson number one on Otherwhere. The one they couldn't give you back at Space Arm because you didn't have the experience."

"Yes, boss. I'll be right back." With a brave smile, the other woman disappeared into the head.

"Well, we sure did a great job on that one, didn't we?"

Andrew shook his head. "We were so happy at how well we were handling it."

"We've got to get something going. We have to find a way to fix this."

Then he slapped his head. "Oh, my god!"

"What?"

"The scrubbers!"

"The scrubbers. Of course. I bet she's never been on a Space Arm vessel."

Andrew looked around. "And here we are, with everything metallic grey and insipid beige and the purest air we can create. She must feel terrible."

"*Diablo.*"

"*Yes, Andrew?*"

"Can you find a scrubber setting you would use if you were throwing a party on board?"

"*What kind of a party?*"

"You have settings for different parties?"

"*Of course: intimate dinner for two, raucous after-game sports party, dignified formal soirée...*

"No, no no. Just a friendly gathering for lunch."

"*Okay. There you go.*"

He looked around. "That's it?"

"*It takes a while. I can't create pheromones out of thin air, you know. You have to do that.*"

Toni regarded their surroundings. "Can you warm up the lighting? Add some amber."

"*Like this?*"

"That's better. Cabin temperature up two degrees."

"*Thermostat reset plus two. Five minutes to deploy.*"

"Time on the pheromone levels?"

"*Twenty minutes. You're not providing the raw materials fast enough.*"

"Well, we're not about to do anything to change that."

"*Just saying.*"

Here she comes.

They looked up. A considerably more composed Morissa hesitated in the doorway.

Toni grinned. "You look much better. Come in and sit down for a drink. Punjabi cinnamon chai, isn't it?"

"Yes. *Diablo* knows how I like it."

"Well, you've got one friend on board, anyway. She never makes my coffee strong enough."

"It's not good for your constitution to drink that muck you make."

"Listen, Tin Can. Go ahead and Mumbot Andrew all you like, but I drink what I want."

"How did you know that?"

"Know what?"

"About Mariel."

Toni shrugged. "Stands to reason. Freighty wanted to look after Andrew, whose real mother is the model for Mumbot part of Freighty. She's part of you, too, isn't she, *Diablo*?"

"I don't know what you mean."

Andrew chuckled. "Toni, I think you've hit on something. I wonder if my real Mum is now an integral part of Freighty's persona."

"I don't know how his excuse for a mind works, but it could be." She looked at the puzzled face of their guest. "Sorry, Morissa, but this is a fascinating new idea for us. Mariel was Andrew's birth mother, but it's more complicated than that. I'm sure you'll have some input when we explain it all. Later."

She brought the steaming chai and placed it on the table. "Now. Here's the basics. Otherwhere is not a place for humans. We've never had a humanorm person out here so we have no control specimens, but we suspect that the edgy feeling we get comes from our augments. Organic augments seem to be affected more. Do you have any organics?"

"No, just the standard academic memory implant."

"Well, I'd say it was interacting as well."

Toni was thinking. "Or it's nothing to do with that part of our brains at all."

Andrew shook his head. "Caught up too much in my own theories. Thanks for that, Toni."

Morissa snorted. "Something is sure interacting."

"Those of us with organic implants can counteract it by social contact. Unfortunately for you, most of that sharing happens over our augments, leaving you out. Does this sound right, Andrew? You're the augment man."

He leaned forward. "Morissa, you could provide good data for my research, if you didn't mind. It's completely non-invasive. Just interviews and opinions."

"Certainly." A faint smile. "I've asked enough people to let me pry into their lives. I can hardly refuse."

"Say, that gives me an idea…"

"Wait a minute, Andrew. Before you go haring off after research material, we're dealing with Morissa, here. Now, we've adjusted the environment slightly. Can you tell?"

The woman frowned. "I think so. It's…warmer. More pleasant. More…friendly." She set her cup down and stared at Toni. "How did you do that?"

"Just like you said. Warmer temperature, warmer light. Pleasant attention from concerned friends. It all helps. Don't worry. We only have three more weeks in Otherwhere and then we'll be back in normal space, and it will all seem like a bad dream."

"I'm looking forward to that."

"And we have to reorganize our social interactions."

Morissa's face brightened. "Of course. You know, I'm supposed to be an expert on this. I've spent day after day analyzing the interactions of groups and tribes and the needs and reasons for them. I never thought of applying it to myself."

Andrew chuckled. "I know what you mean. I've got the opposite problem. I'm the main subject of my own research. My stuff all applies to me, and sometimes nobody else."

She stared at him. "How fascinating. We must have a conversation."

He spread his hands. "I think I can find time in my busy schedule."

Morissa regarded each of them. "This is going to work out, isn't it? The worst is over, and we'll solve this. No problem!"

"No, Morissa." Toni laid her hand over the other woman's. "You haven't come down yet from the adrenaline of your emotions a moment ago. There will still be times when you wake up in the night and wonder if you can make it to the end. But if that happens, you get up and talk to somebody. If nobody's awake, cuddle up to a cat. Otherwhere doesn't seem to bother them. You don't have to fight through alone."

"Um...I didn't want to tell you, but..."

"You don't like cats. Don't worry, we already figured that."

"I'm sorry. I don't dislike them. I just don't know what to do with them."

"Well, let me give you a hint. If you want to get to know one, start with Chakka."

"Chakka? But he's so big. At least Nzinga looks sort of cuddly..."

"And she's the bossiest thing this side of a drill sergeant. You stick to Chakka. He's just an old sweetheart."

Morissa did not look convinced, but she nodded. "It would be worth a try."

"And remember these two are being shipped out here for the same reason you are. They're an integral part of the barwolf team. Consider it part of your duties to get to know them."

"I never thought of it that way. Of course. I'll make regular contact with Chakka until I get used to him. Then maybe I can start on Nzinga. She sounds like the interesting one, actually."

"Oh, she's interesting, all right.

"Ladies, is this crisis over?"

They shared a glance.

"I suppose so."

"May I introduce a new topic of conversation?"

Toni grinned at Morissa. "Brace yourself. Here comes the science."

"No, I'm serious. Morissa's augment — or something — is interacting with Otherwhere. She has no communication abilities. Ergo, the communication element of the augments is not what causes the interaction with Otherwhere."

"Unless it is the natural human ability to communicate through otherwise that is creating the interaction."

"Which looks more and more possible, and now I have someone to use as a control."

Toni shrugged and glanced at Morissa, turning the conversation over to her.

"As I said before, Andrew. I'm all yours for the next two months."

"Yes, but we're only in Otherwhere for three more weeks. I've gotta get moving." He pointed a finger at her. "You. You're the social scientist. You can help me design the tests."

She laughed. "I suppose so, but the veiled-purpose questions I make up won't be very useful for testing myself."

"What's a veiled-purpose question?"

"Well, here's how it works..."

Toni slipped away, leaving them deep in statistical analysis, a topic in which she had no interest. Her philosophy was much more in line with the Space Commando's Test. "If it moves, shoot it. If it doesn't move, hide behind it."

Image: Nzinga chasing small, four-legged creature across landscape.

Image: Chakka poking at small, four-legged creature. Finally it runs, and he chases it across landscape.

I get it. The Auguar's Test. If it moves, chase it. If it doesn't move, prod it until it moves. Then chase it.

Image: feline laughter.

8. FREIGHTY IN RE-TI

At day 40 of their trip they flipped over to decel, allowing Morissa another brief time to enjoy weightlessness. She was having such a good time that Andrew started an impromptu game of G-free volleyball in the lounge and rescheduled the start of the long deceleration to the Barnard System.

Now they were only one light year from the factory, and Otherwhere communication with Freighty had shorter and shorter delay times. When the lag approached ten minutes, it was more effective to dispense with the avatar and speak directly, as if they were sending com texts.

Freighty's first comments on the barwolves proved his worth. "It would be useful to investigate the population control mechanisms of the subjects. Have you discovered any other predators on the planet? You mentioned specifically that the vast number of subjects appeared to be in good health. I have been monitoring the new data coming in from the research team downplanet, and their observations have not come up with anything different."

Andrew looked at Morissa, a frown on his brow. "How can that work? What usually limits the population?"

She counted on her fingers. "Predators, disease, food supply, war."

"War?"

"Do the math. Those societies in Ancient Earth where one man could have four or more wives? None of the other statistics change. What happened to all the extra men?"

Andrew's face blanked a moment. "Right. Those were some of the most warlike societies. The rich old men sent the poor young ones off to get killed so they could keep the leftover women to themselves."

Morissa frowned. "I couldn't have said it better myself. And if you look at more recent Human history, you'll see that little has changed."

63

Toni shook her head. "According to Captain O'Rourke, all that is changing now. Freighty thinks so, or he wouldn't have contacted us."

"We're back to Freighty. What are we going to answer?"

"You already have. Nothing." Andrew mimicked the finger counting. "No disease, no predators. There seems to be an even spread of Toni's moosey things all across the temperate areas of the planet, so there's no food shortage.

"Right. We'll have to start a survey of them as well."

"The barwolf population seems to have reached the carrying capacity of their chosen environment, and we don't know how they maintain it."

"We need to know more about their heredity." Andrew regarded Morissa. "Can a species have a self-destructive gene that limits its population automatically?"

She shrugged. "I have no idea of the natural selection process that would give rise to it, but we're talking about aliens, here. Why not?"

He tapped a finger on the table. "So, our job will be to find the trigger."

Toni pulled out her sidearm and slid the loading mechanism back, then closed it. "Sounds like good self-preservation."

Andrew leaned over and pretended to whisper to Morissa. "Ignore that annoying little habit. She does it when she's feeling insecure."

A small smile tweaked the other woman's lip. "I've often wondered why she wears that thing in a spaceship in the middle of Otherwhere."

Andrew held up both hands. "Don't answer, Toni. Whatever you say will be absolutely correct, but taken out of context, completely hilarious."

She stared him down. "And that brings us back to the original topic of conversation: war."

Andrew shrugged. "And that's our answer to Freighty?"

"I think so. Let's ask if he has any information on that from other alien species."

The next response took longer to come, but Andrew reassured them. "He has vast databanks. Huge rooms of them, and they are thousands of times more efficient than anything we have. Complete histories of five intelligent species. If he wants to research something thoroughly, it might take him ten or fifteen minutes to find the data, and who knows how long to translate it into Standard English."

When it came, it took half an hour to download.

"This data comes in three sections." Freighty was in his Southern European guise today, and he had picked up the habit of counting on his fingers. "The first is for our present discussion. The second is a selected reading list that Morissa can peruse in the next two months before she starts the job. The rest is esoteric material that you'll probably never use. Once you've become conversant with my cataloguing system, you'll be able to scan the larger volume should you happen to need it."

Morissa was trying valiantly to figure out the menus. "There's a hundred years' worth of reading, here. Can *Diablo's* memory banks hold it all?"

Andrew looked over the download. "The major block is in a compressed form that you won't be able to access onboard. When we get to *Unicorn* they'll be able to store and decode it. At that point, you'll have to deal with Securi-Corps and all sorts of bureaucratic hassles, because it will automatically become restricted material."

Morissa sighed. "Ah, yes. Bureaucracy."

Soon a new message came in. "Oh, and remember that I am running a business."

They stared at the viewscreen.

"I have given you free access to one of my products, which is a huge sign of my approval of your project. However, that material is not in the public domain, and will never be." The avatar gave a smug grin. "Think about it. Intellectual property comes into public ownership seventy-five years after the death of the author, I believe."

Toni gave him a stern frown. "You're saying that some day we're going to have to pay for this help."

They waited for the response, which came with an innocent shrug. "Isn't that how human commercial interactions work? I offer what I have, you take it if you need it."

Andrew chuckled. "Freighty, you learned your sales pitch from our media, which uses statistical probability to sell. Those techniques only have to work on that small percentage of the population that will fall for them. In case you didn't notice, the people you are dealing with are not in that percentage.

"And if you want to know whether the samples are distinguished by relative intelligence, the answer is, 'Not always.' In fact, if someone really wants what you're offering, they will use all of their brainpower to persuade themselves and others that your product is the best possible solution to all their problems. In any case, that's the end of the Social Niceties lecture. What do you think of those photos?"

To open his next message, Freighty lifted a hand with a graceful turn of the wrist. "Well, there you have it. I am appealing to people who need my products.

"But to business. The behaviour is a poser, all right. At first glance it looks completely irrational. I've dealt with aggressive species before. The ones that wiped out my creators were a ferocious race, quite capable of a slaughter like this, and of their own species as well. It happened several times that I know of, on a vast scale. One thing I can tell you, there was always a reason for it."

Freighty gave a wry smile. "In that respect, they were more civilized than humans. They were very intelligent and practical. There was no killing for sport or pleasure. They would consider that many deaths to be a waste of resources, to be sacrificed only if the long-term results warranted it. What were the long-term results of this battle, Miss Goodall? Do you have any evidence of this sort of occurrence happening elsewhere?"

Andrew looked to Morissa to send an answer.

"We haven't had any feedback yet. In the short term all the packs returned to their own grounds and went back to their normal habits. We don't know if a new pack will form or if the territory will be annexed by one or several of the neighbours. We'll be watching developments in that region carefully."

Andrew nodded. "We have instructed our foragers to keep an eye open. They used the opportunity to gather tissue samples, so we'll get an idea of how long it takes the bones and external plating to decompose. Fossil evidence is a long way down the line, I'm afraid."

They chatted about the situation while they waited for the return message, but no one had anything further to add.

Finally, Freighty's image came through again. "It sounds like you'll be gathering a great deal of useful information in the near future. Please keep me in the loop. Space travel is rather eventless. Is that a word?"

"I could theorize, if you like." He stroked his chin. "Let's assume that this is not an isolated incident. If this sort of thing happens frequently in their society, then it has some function. Wars are usually a way of thinning out overpopulation, for example."

Andrew grinned as he composed his answer. "Eventless is not an everyday word, but it gets the message across. I would have thought that war as a population control device would mean larger swings of growth and depletion, more like a plague works."

Morissa nodded. "But all the evidence we have so far indicates a fairly stable population level. It will take years to chart the natural swings, of course. It's difficult to tell with an alien species, but all the individuals we have seen have conformed to a certain standard of strength, speed, and body shape. This indicates a large number of healthy individuals."

"More and more puzzling," Andrew chipped in, "the even spreading of the population is a further indication of stability. The planet has little axial tilt, so seasonal migration is not a factor."

"Everything on this planet reeks of stability. Then this happens. I don't know."

When Freighty came back on he shook his head. "I notice that as this conversation becomes less creative and more chatty, you find the time lag more irksome. Perhaps it would better be handled by my avatar in your system." The image shivered and resumed with little difference that Toni could tell. Perhaps slightly less fluidity of motion.

He smiled at Morissa. "They didn't bring Earth's foremost expert out here because everything was going to be normal and easy, did they? A bureaucrat could have handled that."

"The world's foremost expert in a field of one."

"Well, you have an experienced, talented, and well-equipped team. I have every confidence in you."

"Well...ah...thank you, sir. I hope I can live up to your expectations."

"How are you holding up to Otherwhere?"

"Um...I don't know any standard to judge by."

Freighty grinned. "Good answer. My observation has been that humans who have little problem with Otherwhere tend to be at the less sensitive end of the scale."

"Oh." She afforded him a faint smile. "Is this where I tell you about the crying spells and the sleepless nights?"

"Oh, I already know about those."

Toni took pity on Morissa's shocked expression. "He has a little birdy that tells him everything."

"That's right. I wasn't asking about your symptoms. I wanted to know how you felt about them. It sounds like you're willing to accept them as part of the hardship of the assignment, and carry on regardless."

"Oh! Oh...yes, I suppose that's the way I look at it."

He smiled again. "Good. We'll be in close enough contact to have re-ti conversations in the next few days. Let's do some thinking and talk again tomorrow. Maybe you'll get some more data relayed in, and we can go over it."

"Thank you, sir. I'd like that."

"Please call me Freighty. 'Sir' sounds far too military for me."

"All right, Freighty."

The avatar included the others in his glance. "Anything else I need to know before I dump this scintillating dialogue to the real Freighty?"

Andrew waved a hand. "Nothing important. I'll upload the latest tests on Toni and me as soon as I've looked them over."

"Nothing spectacular going on there, I gather?"

"Nope. Steady progress in the right direction, pretty much as expected."

"How disappointing. I was hoping for fireworks and flashing lights."

Andrew dropped his chin and put on a plummy accent. "Very unscientific, old boy. Slow and steady, that's the pace."

"When I'm headed in the opposite direction at zero point eight Lights, I would prefer not to hear the word, 'slow,' if you don't mind."

9.MEETING IN SPACE

Diablo slipped out of Otherwhere when she reached the appropriate speed and went into her usual deceleration. Days passed, and the re-ti routine of the ship settled everyone's nerves. Morissa was caught up in her research of Freighty's materials and kept them entertained at dinner every night with snippets of scientific fact or supposition she had found during the day.

Toni continued to train Nzinga in everything she could think of that might help with the coming operations, and also with the standard material they had missed by graduating early. A lot of this involved training in security and electronics, and they roamed *Diablo's* circuits, cataloguing, learning and doing standard maintenance checks, while trying bery hard not to mess anything up.

Until the day they blew the galley circuits. They were in the middle of a standard penetration protocol when the whole system crashed. A cascading series of overloads spread too rapidly for even two minds to control, and all they could do was withdraw.

When it was over, they sat in the dark, shaken.

What the hell was that?

Emotion: abject apology.

No, it was my fault. We must have missed something. But what?

Then Andrew slid into their gestalt uninvited. *Oops. Now, how did that happen?*

Toni was instantly suspicious. *What do you mean?*

Emotion: indifference. Looks like somebody wasn't careful enough.

We were being very careful! I don't know what went wrong.

Emotion: sly humour. Then I suggest you find out and fix it, or it's going to be a cold, dark supper tonight.

His image disappeared.

Image: Captain standing over small auguar, scowling. Emotion: contrition and fear.

Toni had her own frown. *Emotion: denial. We were set up, Pumpkin. This is a test. We have to get back in there, figure out what kind of booby-trap he left and fix it.*

Emotion: question?

He set us up. Let's go back to the point it all went south and see what we find. We entered the air-con system last time, so now we'll go in through fire suppression. He won't have messed with that.

Emotion: determination.

Atta girl. Dig in!

It took a while, but finally they found it: a classic trick. One line of code in a safety check had a missing semicolon, meaning that the instruction to turn on the system was ignored. Knowing that the safeguard was already turned off meant that you didn't have to turn it off to access the system.

Crap. So instead we turned the alarm on and blundered right in. Let's get at it, kid. We have a bunch of circuits to turn on. We'll have to check them all, now, in case he left any other presents for us.

Soon the lights were back on, the vents were blowing warm air and life looked rosy again. But the incident got Toni thinking, and after she finished her supper, she pushed her plate away and regarded Andrew. "When we're practising our attacks and penetrations, why don't we ever run into any of *Diablo's* security? I assume she has the best Freighty could design."

"She does. But you'll never see it."

"How does that work?"

"Because the security network doesn't run in the same circuits as the rest of the ship. There's a parallel metasystem that doesn't use electricity, on non-metallic ubercircuits that are almost impossible to detect."

"How does it work?"

"You and Nzinga come into the galley system with me again."

They entered through the lighting this time, and soon their gestalt showed the circuitry.

"See these cutouts every once in a while?"

"Yes, they're spare junctions in case of retrofits and add-ons." She glanced at his grin. "They aren't, are they?"

"Well, they are. But they're also access points to the metasystem. Every time an impulse comes through that node, it has to bounce into the ubercircuits for verification. It's then tagged and sent on. If there's an interruption between two nodes, the verification is nullified and the impulse stops. Then the metasystem takes over and starts checking to see what happened."

"What if it's a false alarm?"

"It usually is: a fault in a circuit or a clash with another sub-routine. If the meta finds that, it either fixes it or flags it for maintenance. If it finds an intrusion of some sort, all the bells and whistles start sounding, and the antivirus programs flood the area. It's very much like the human immune system but more complex and far more reliable."

"That explains a lot. Thanks."

"No problem. What's the next system in danger of small, sharp, mental claws?"

"We're working on the laser targetting system tomorrow. Don't start a war without giving us due warning, okay?"

"You're supposed to be able to do this work on a fully functioning system without anyone noticing."

"We'll be working on that aspect as well." Toni and Nzinga returned to their task with renewed diligence, and the days passed swiftly.

* * *

They cruised in high over the Oort Cloud and increased decel to account for the growing pull of Barnard's Star. Messages from Freighty were now stretching to weeks, and communication with the Barnard Embassy becoming days, then hours for a turnaround. A feeling of optimism filled the little ship.

Toni continued to observe their passenger, but with less concern. Given time to digest the data she was receiving on a daily basis now, the scientist was able to settle into her working routines.

Andrew, on the other hand, was getting less settled. Never one for sitting around, he was now showing every evidence of needing his next project.

To be fair, Toni wasn't exactly enthused about playing the serious senior officer role. They were headed for an exciting assignment, and she, too, was anxious to get started.

So, when he insisted for about the thirteenth time that they run a set of augment isolation drills that she had mastered three days ago, she knew he was just bored, and said so.

He surveyed her face with a smirk. "And you, a tyro who has only received her full organics in the past year, can tell what I, the acknowledged expert in two star systems, intend to do with this data?"

Toni regarded his smile. "Do you know what the term 'insufferable' means?"

He went into augment just long enough that he had to be faking. "I had to look it up. It is so far removed from my cooperative, amiable nature as to be a completely foreign concept."

"Thus demonstrating complete understanding. Do you know there's one stage worse than insufferable?"

"Please tell me. I'll work on it."

"It's being unsufferable on purpose. You're already an expert."

"Well, that leaves me with a challenge, doesn't it?"

She shook her head. "*Diablo,* can you think of a maintenance job that would require the captain spend at least four hours EV?"

"*Sorry, ma'am. All external systems are running at optimal.*"

"*Couldn't you create something?*"

"*Of course, but I'd have to run it by the captain first.*"

"*Diablo, are you aware of the term insufferable?*"

"*Anything to keep my crew happy and entertained, ma'am.*"

73

Toni jumped to her feet and went over to the exterior wall of the lounge.

"What are you doing?"

"I'm getting out the exercise machine. I feel the need to let off some steam."

Morissa raised her head from her reader. "Are you two always like this?"

Andrew turned wide blue eyes on her. "Like what?"

"How do you ever manage to get along in a spaceship for months at a time?"

"We can't. That's why you're here. We made up a job for you in the Barnard System so we'd have a referee for the trip out."

"Huh." She returned to her reader, then looked up. "And knowing you like I do now, that just might be partially true."

Diablo, Diablo, Diablo. This is Barnard Embassy calling Diablo.

All three humans froze, heads turned towards the viewscreen.

This is Diablo, Barnard Embassy. How can we help you?

They waited in anticipation while the message winged its way through millions of kilometres of space.

You can put your captain on the blower, please, Diablo.

Andrew checked his augment. "That's a secure line. I'll take it on the bridge. Toni, you'll probably want to hear this as well."

When they were seated on the accel couches, Andrew activated the bridge com on external feed.

"Captain Collingwood here, Barnard Embassy."

Image: com room on the Unicorn. Sergeant Jackson onscreen.

"Hi, Andrew. How's the trip going?"

At this stage the com lag had shrunk to a mildly annoying few minutes, so the conversation went relatively smoothly.

"Fine, Jackson. Good to talk to you re-ti, sort of. What's happening in Barnard's that I need to know about?"

"New orders for you from the boss."

"Which boss would that be?"

74

"Whichever one you want. They just talked it over. Your Mum is out in the Oort cloud investigating...something-or-other. Coincidentally, her position is right along your course and she's heading back to base any time, now."

"I see. And all I have to do is adjust my route closer to the ecliptic and hit the brakes a little harder, and we'll end up side by side. Coincidentally, almost."

"I can see your navigation skills are up to par, kid. And those are your new orders. Get through to *NightHawk* on the channel I'm sending you and arrange it."

"Good enough. Anything else, Jackson?"

"Nope. Just 'Welcome home' from all of us."

"Good to be back. See you in a week."

"See you then."

Andrew closed down the radio and glanced over at Toni. "Rescue is at hand."

She grinned. "Do you think that's the objective?"

"Probably not, but every little bit counts. *NightHawk's* crew is probably ready for some new faces, as well." He was setting the radio up. "Interesting that it's a security channel, though. There's a reason for that."

Toni shrugged. "I'll leave the suspicion up to you. She's your mother, and you're the only one I know that can figure out what she really wants. I find it easier to just follow her orders. She's good at those, too."

"And that's what we're doing. Wanna go tell our passenger about the early finish to her purgatory?" He turned back to the radio, and Toni slid out of her accel couch and headed for the mess lounge, where Morissa was still working.

"Well, good news on the radio."

The scientist looked up. Her face was less drawn, and the shadows under her eyes had receded. "Good news is always...well...good news. Make my day."

"I hope you're in the process of wrapping up any projects you're working on, because our solitude just got shortened by about five days."

"How's that? Did Barnard's Star take a jump in our direction?"

"No, but the long arm of the Barnard Ambassador has reached out and tweaked our course. We rendezvous with *NightHawk* in a couple of days. Think of it. New company, real chairs, and a professional cook. Jonny's pavlova is legendary." She regarded the scientist. "You don't look exactly enthused."

Morissa shrugged. "I was just getting used to you two. Now there's going to be a whole new bunch of people to distract me. You're right. If I want to get anything finished, I'd better get at it now."

Toni re-evaluated the situation. "Don't worry. You'll still be able to come out here for peace of mind. *Diablo* matches up to *NightHawk's* airlock, and we just ride along."

The other woman smiled up at her. "Don't think I'm antisocial, Toni. I just like new people in small doses."

"This will break you in easy. There's usually ten crew on *NightHawk,* and they're spread pretty thin, with sleeping and duty watches. A week from now you'll be at the embassy, where there's about a thousand residents plus the two hundred crewmembers on each of five destroyers, who rotate to the civilization of the station for their shore leave."

"Hmm. And here I pictured the Outback as this sparsely-populated expanse where you could go for a week and never see anyone."

"It is. But the old *Unicorn* was 300 metres long and 60 metres in diameter, with a full battle complement of 1500 souls. Now that it's not a functioning carrier, there's all sorts of room inside, and that's a good thing. From what I hear, there's new ships arriving insystem on a weekly basis. Some official, some not, but they're coming, and they have to be taken care of."

"You mean kept under control."

"Works both ways."

Morissa frowned. "And all those people are functioning on food brought from Earth?"

"Every ship uses hydroponics to create food and refresh the air, but yes, most of the food is freeze-dried and sent from Earth."

"A problem for the barwolves, then."

"Oh, yes. There will be farmers with greedy eyes. Another pressure point for you."

The scientist shook her head. "I find a new one every day. And Captain O'Rourke will probably add to the load. Any ideas?"

"Not a clue. Maybe she'll relieve some of them. Just remember, she's on our side."

"Which side is 'our side'? Remember, I'm supposed to be impartial."

Toni grinned. "Space Arm is also impartial, as is Freighty. We're the ones that want everything to be done right, by the rules. You can count on it."

Morissa was silent for a while. Finally, she looked up. "I suppose eventually I'll have to trust someone."

Toni's heart went out to the other woman. She sat beside her. "You've chosen a very lonely job. You're cut off from almost everyone through no fault of your own. First because of your judicial duty. Second because you're a monogen. Third because you're that sort of person.

"I went through this in the Commandos. Sooner or later you just have to make friends. You have to figure out who's on your side and make a decision to stand by them. It's a tough phase, but once you find yourself working with a team you can relax, and you actually get more done."

Morissa smiled. "Thanks, Toni. I'd like to think I made a start with you and Andrew." She glanced over to the side of the room. "Maybe even Chakka. He stays down here with me sometimes, and I talk to him."

"He's been around people a few years. He sort of understands human speech. Not so much with Nzinga, yet?"

"Oh, I think she tolerates me, poor deaf-and-dumb creature that I am."

Toni had a thought. "Have you ever thought of getting an augment?"

"How would I do that, out here?"

"There's a well-qualified surgical team at the embassy to do augment maintenance for all the Space Arm personnel. Let's talk to Andrew about this." She looked at the frown starting to appear. "You can't really do a good job of assessing the barwolves when you have no idea what their communications feel like."

"No, I suppose you're right. Let's talk to Andrew. He's the specialist, after all." She gave Toni a puzzled look. "How do you work with that, anyway? He's only...what...just turning seventeen years old, and quite frankly, sometimes he acts like it. But he's the captain of this ship and a top specialist in the Space Arm scientific community. Also, he's an ensign and you're his superior officer."

The commando shook her head. "You're asking the wrong person. Half the time I don't know how I feel about him or how to treat him." Then she grinned. "But I have one touchstone. If I ever wonder what to do about him, I just remember what his mother would do to me if I ever let him come to harm. That usually answers all my questions."

* * *

Andrew's response about the augment was a shrug. "Of course, I think you should get one. You can ask my Mum, and she'll say the same. But she'll tell you to ask the ambassador. Alfino's your boss, isn't he?"

"I suppose he must be. There wasn't much time before I left to get that sort of thing straight."

"Well, you'll have to talk to him about everything, because he's the main man around this system. More power than any monarch Earth every produced." He grinned, "To hear him talk, he's hemmed in by rules and regulations and considerations on all sides, but that's a good thing. Those restrictions would keep a less intelligent or less moral man from making big mistakes."

"You have a high opinion of him?"

Andrew regarded her. "I've watched you worry for this whole trip as you found out more and more about what you've got yourself into. I went through that when I arrived with *Diablo*. What I figured out is the other side of the equation. There's a very high-powered and right-minded group of people out here, ready and willing to help. It balances."

"That's funny." She pointed a finger at Toni. "She just said the same thing."

"Therefore, given the small number of entities in this environment, it must be universally true."

"In this environment."

He grinned. "Baby steps. You're going to be on board your greatest asset in two days."

"*NightHawk?*"

"Yeah. I'm sure you heard the story about how the interplanetaries used the *Clyde* to boss everyone around because it was the biggest, meanest kid on the block. Well, up to now, Space Arm has had the *NightHawk* in the same role. Alfino rules the 'hood, and Mum and her ship are his enforcers."

"And they're all on my side."

"Yep. Just keep that in mind tomorrow when you're inundated with the load of reprobates she keeps as crew."

"Reprobates."

"Yeah. Toughest bunch of commandos in the Arm. Wouldn't have been given their positions if they hadn't been. Look at Toni. She's the cream of the crop."

Morissa glanced at Toni, whose face felt hot under the scrutiny.

"But she's...so nice. She's been a good friend to me."

"Yeah. Tell that to the three goons that tried to rape one of her classmates."

"Three?"

"Yeah. She never drew her weapon because she wanted to keep the incident under wraps. She sent one to hospital and just beat the other two up."

"Oh."

Toni didn't know where to look. She pulled out her sidearm and began to disassemble it, but her fingers weren't as steady as usual.

"Yeah. So, if you're having trouble being underwhelmed by the sparkling personalities of my former crewmates, just tell yourself that they're all 'nice.' Just like Toni."

* * *

Toni stomped into the mess area and went straight to the exercise machine. "Andrew, I want to do some of those doubles drills."

"Any special reason?"

"Emotional misdirection. I need to get my hands on you, and the only other option is a sparring session where I wouldn't guarantee your safety."

He grinned. "Exercise it is, then. I always prefer cooperation to confrontation."

"Sure, as long as everyone is cooperating with you." She started pulling levers.

I wouldn't set up that equipment right now if I were you, ma'am.

"Since you're hardly likely ever to be me, that's a moot point, *Diablo.* Why?"

"Rendezvous with NightHawk in forty minutes, ma'am."

Toni glanced at Andrew. "And once again your mother saves your butt at the last moment."

He favoured her with his best smirk, but then reached out and ruffled her hair.

I know what he's doing. Damn him, he knows it works. She slapped his hand away, faked a one-two to his solar plexus, and went to prepare for docking.

The linkup with *NightHawk* took a while, because *Diablo* had to disengage her external fuel tank and attach it to the port side of the mothership's bow before she moored herself alongside on starboard. But finally the airlock opened, revealing a uniformed but highly disorganized reception committee.

Andrew and Chakka vaulted across the gravity change as if they had been doing it all their lives, leaving the three females to make their way in more dignified fashion.

The lad threw himself into the captain's arms. "Mother, mother, thank you, oh, thank you."

She finished the hug, then stood him up and stared at him. "That was an unusual display of emotion. To what do I attribute this unusual gratitude?"

"You have saved me from another five days alone with these women."

Natalia glanced at Toni. "Well, I know from experience that you won't stand for his tricks." She turned and held out a hand to Morissa. "Dr. Goodall, I'm sorry you had to put up with him for so long. I'm glad to see you figured out how to treat him."

Morissa shook the captain's hand firmly. "And from what I've heard about you, I expect you're immediately going to tune him up and transform him into the perfect ensign."

"Oh, no. I never do that in public. Not good for my image or my status with the crew." She glanced around at the crowded hallway. "Don't stand on ceremony, you lot. We've been a long time without a new face or an old one over again. Get into the mess hall and crack the keg."

Turning her back on the crew, she gave Toni a hug that lifted the other woman's feet off the floor.

Meanwhile the other *NightHawks* were crowding around Andrew, giving him a rough-and-tumble welcome.

Natalia glanced over at the melee, then put an arm across each woman's shoulders. "That'll keep them busy for a while. Come up to the chart room for a debrief."

As they loped up the slideway forward, she spoke aloud. "*NightHawk,* give that mob due warning and then hit one G for the embassy."

Warning all. One G acceleration in thirty seconds from my mark. Mark.

Natalia grinned. "Just enough time for us to get sitting down. Come on in."

There was an extra chair beside the desk, and the captain motioned Morissa to sit there. Toni took the stool and signalled to Nzinga, who gladly retreated to Chakka's bed under the desk.

The captain sat, glancing down. "When is she going to notice me?"

Toni smiled. "When you deign to notice her. She's rather overwhelmed at the moment. She is used to being the queen of all she surveys. To come on board this ship and meet two new people she must look up to is quite a shock."

"Two?"

"Lundeen. He's the functional master of this little universe, and everyone on the ship agrees. And look at your position. It never occurred to her little mind that there might be someone whom I look up to as she looks up to me. Sort of makes you a god."

"I never thought to ask. How do she and Chakka get along?"

"In human terms, like an uncle and a favoured niece. She gets to be the boss as long as she doesn't disagree with him. Which she is careful never to do."

The captain's eyes went to her other guest. "So, Dr. Goodall, has three months in a tin can with this menagerie warped you for life?"

The other woman smiled. "Let's say it has changed my outlook in many ways, most of them good, some of them a bit scary."

"That sounds about right. A gentle introduction to the Outback."

"You call that gentle? Now, that's really scary."

The captain leaned back in her chair. "Well, we're missing out on the start of a well-earned party, but just before we go down to the celebrations, is there anything on your mind I can ease, first thing?"

"Actually, something came up today. I only have the standard academic implant. Toni suggests I should consider an augment."

"So, Toni and Andrew think you should get one, but Andrew referred you to me, saying that I'd probably pass the buck to Dr. Pretoro, because he's your boss."

"Oh. They already told you?"

"No, that's how they think. They're a wonderfully independent pair except where it comes to me, and they know the limits of my authority."

"But you think I should get one."

Natalia grinned. "Not letting me duck out, are you? Of course I do. It was only the big rush to get someone with academic authority out here that made them choose someone as inappropriate as you are." She held up a cautioning hand. "But only because of the augment, and that's easily solvable."

"Not quite that easy, ma'am." Toni touched her own neck, just below the ear.

"Not? Oh, the organics. Of course. They have to develop...organically, don't they?"

"Yes, and we've only been speculating, but we assume there will be time pressures on Morissa's decision."

"There already are, and they are building." The captain steepled her fingers. "Maybe I'm speaking out of turn here, but nothing I've seen recently has changed my original analysis. Dr. Goodall, I'm sure you realize that you will be dealing with the only other oxycarb planet within many light years of earth. Altruism and morals aside, there is no chance in this universe that people will not go and live there. Do you understand that?"

"I can't let that sway my decision, whatever it turns out to be."

The Natalia nodded. "A laudable resolve. But you may come to the point where, no matter what your scientific decision is regarding the intelligence of the barwolves, you have to throw your weight behind the faction whose plans result in the best chance the barwolf society has to survive and develop in any natural way on a planet they share with a large human population. Now, that may not happen for a hundred years, but it will happen."

She slapped the table. "But I am way ahead of myself. Dr. Pretoro will be very angry with me if I bring him a scientific expert who is already indoctrinated." She smiled. "I'm just putting you alongside Jane Goodall. She spent the first few years of her career doing exactly what you will be doing: deciding how intelligent her clients were. Then she spent the rest of her life trying to make sure her clients survived."

Morissa gave the captain a level gaze. "I can see worse ways to spend one's life."

"Oh, no. That's not my point. I believe that if you go in from the start knowing what the end objective is, you'll be more likely to succeed. Jane Goodall was always fighting from behind. Always trying to right wrongs from centuries of mismanagement. You can be in front. Never forget that."

The scientist winced. "Bad science, good politics."

"Right. And the best politics you can play right now is to be a good scientist. So don't listen to me. Let's go down and see what wine Jonny has decided on for this special homecoming."

The party went on for several hours, until Toni could see that Morissa was exhausted. She extricated her from a conversation with Chief Engineer Lundeen about the Lapps of Finland and toted her off to *Diablo.*

"Let's not overdo it the first day back in society. You'll want to sleep late tomorrow. Jonny can provide breakfast any time of the day, and Andrew already transferred some of your chai across.

"When did he have time to do that?"

"I keep telling you. The lad's a logistics wizard."

Jane yawned. "Remind me to thank him tomorrow."

"You won't see him up early. I heard him trying to persuade the crew into a poker game."

"Fools. But you're right. Nice ones." Goodall closed her cabin door, and Toni returned to the party, determined to keep her bets very low. It was worth the price of admission just to watch him play.

* * *

The next morning, she managed to drag herself out of bed with the help of a cold, damp nose that kept inserting itself under her blanket.

"All right, all right. I know you want a quick run around that beautiful track. Give me a moment to wake up."

By the time they hit the perimeter track on *NightHawk's* rotational pod, Andrew and Chakka were already at full speed, and Fiona and Charlie were trying to match them. She rolled into the stream, feeling the pickup of a friendly cadre, and was soon loping along comfortably.

"Nice to get some real exercise again."

Fiona glanced over. "What do you have for workout on that little thing?"

"Oh, there's an amazing foldaway machine that takes up about half the empty space in the mess, then disappears into the bulkhead. But it's not the same as running and going somewhere."

They both chuckled at the irony, then jogged on.

After breakfast she asked permission from the captain to explore *NightHawk's* circuitry with Nzinga, as a training exercise.

"We've been using *Diablo,* but so much of that ship is wired to Freighty's specifications that there's very little standard stuff left."

"How does that work?"

"Chakka leads a course through the system, and Nzinga has to follow. He leaves clues she has to pick up like a treasure hunt."

Natalia waved a hand in the direction of the central column where the ArIn was housed. "Be my guest. I trust you won't break anything."

"Oh, we're trained to be very careful with the circuits that are keeping us alive."

"Glad to hear it."

The next day she heard Fiona, the Second Engineer, complaining to the Chief about a problem she was having.

"I just can't figure it, Nelson. I've known the security systems on this ship since she came out of space dock. This morning I went to do a routine sweep of the secondary thermostatic damper system, because it gets used more in Otherwhere, and I wanted to see that there hadn't been any wear and tear.

"I couldn't get in. There were a bunch of false leads installed, and once I sorted those out, I got caught in a logic trap that threatened to crash the whole system."

Lundeen frowned. "I haven't been anywhere near the dampers since we shut them down when we came back into Realspace."

"Yeah, well that wasn't all. I pulled out and went to check the manuals to see what to do about it. Took me about half an hour. When I went back into the system, the bugs had all disappeared. For the life of me I couldn't tell that anything had ever been wrong." She tossed her hands up. "I just can't figure it."

"Did you ask *NightHawk?*"

"*NightHawk* wasn't very helpful, actually. Just said not to worry about it."

"Well, maybe we'd better ask *NightHawk* again. I don't like the sound of this."

Toni cleared her throat. "...would that have been part of the Otherwhere heat dissipation system?"

"Yes. Why?"

"I...don't think you need to worry about it."

"I don't?" The dark woman frowned. "What do you know about the heat exchangers?"

"Personally, I don't know anything about them. But Chakka was running an obstacle course for Nzinga, and we needed an electronic field that the ship wasn't using."

"Obstacle course?"

"He goes into the system and lays a trail with traps and feedback loops and anything else he can think of. She has to go in and follow the spoor and wipe it out. Put it all back to normal."

"But what if the ship needed that system in the middle of their game?"

"That's the whole point of electronic espionage. The system has to work perfectly through the whole exercise, despite the modifications. When they're finished, it's exactly the way it was before. No harm done. In fact, they do a complete maintenance sweep when they're done, and the system is then better than ever. That way Nzinga learns the anti-sabotage techniques and becomes familiar with standard ship's systems at the same time."

The captain stepped into the room, aware as usual when anything was going on. "What do you think of that, Nelson? Any harm in it?"

He shook his head. "I can't complain about Chakka doing a maintenance sweep of the ship's systems, especially ones that aren't being used. In fact, it explains an elevated draw I noticed on the spare parts files in the last couple of days. I'm not sure I'm so happy about the espionage games. What if they left something behind?"

Natalia grinned. "This is Chakka we're talking about. Can you see him leaving tufts of cat hair in the resistors?"

"Couldn't they practise on the *Diablo* instead?"

Toni shook her head. "We've already used all the standard equipment on the IOR, but too much of that is Freighty's custom work. It's less useful for training purposes, and we don't know it as well, so there is more chance of an error."

The captain considered. "I suggest you coordinate with Engineering on their standard maintenance schedule and play your little spy games as part of the usual checks. Will that work?"

Lundeen nodded, and Toni shrugged. "Sort of takes the spontaneity out of the lesson, but I guess we'll manage."

The Chief Engineer frowned. "You mess up our propulsion system out here a thousand AUs from the middle of nowhere, and things are going to get a whole lot more spontaneous than you bargained for."

"No argument, Chief. We'll stay out of Life Support, too."

Lundeen reached over and rubbed the top of Nzinga's head. "You have no idea how good that makes me feel."

She accepted his homage with a queenly purr.

* * *

There were no more untoward incidents, and *NightHawk* swooped down beside the Inner Asteroid Belt in tip-top maintenance. The *Unicorn* had taken up orbit at Lagrange 4 downspin of Xeta, Freighty's former refuge orbiting between the two belts. The old carrier was losing its shape as a ship and gaining the gantries, external walkways and solar panel arrays of a permanent space station. A closer view showed swarms of various small ships buzzing merrily in and out of the work bays. One of the destroyers, the *Ontario,* was moored outside the main repair dock, and the *Nevada* was standing off waiting her turn.

Toni regarded the scene on the forward viewscreens. "Busy place. Where did all this population come from?"

Natalia grinned. "Just like usual. Once the hostilities were over, everyone who was lying low suddenly appeared. We've also had two small colony ships from earth already. There's no way they could have organized that so quickly. One of them was an old sublight planetary colonizer. It was thirty years getting here! Word was out long before we came and opened the can of worms."

"I don't see any reason to limit immigration. Anybody with the guts and money to come all this way probably has the moxie to find a niche, and this population is far below the break-even level for a sustainable economy."

The captain sighed. "Oh, I'm sure there will be a sprinkling of dreamers, scammers, and religious evangelists with more ideals than brains. But most of them will survive. Take countries like Canada and Australia. Started out as colonies in hostile wilderness, and look at them now."

The forward section of the carrier had been taken over by the diplomatic wing because it contained the human habitation spaces. *Diablo* and *Night Hawk* slipped in to moor at adjoining personnel hatches. A Space Arm honour guard of three whole Marines, razor-sharp in their whites, met them in the hallway outside the docks and escorted them to the ambassador's reception room, which had most of the fittings, brackets and tracking of its former machine shop configuration removed or disguised.

Andrew glanced around as he entered. "Hey, Dr. Pretoro. Good to see you again. The place looks much better." He shook the offered hand.

The ambassador slapped Andrew on the shoulder, smiling broadly. "Like the new paint job? Glad to have you back. Uneventful trip?"

"Nothing to match what has been happening out here. I'll make a full report later."

"Fine. Hello, Toni. Sorry to pull you out of your little niche at the Academy, but we need your skills."

She smiled and shook his hand. "They were getting tired of my abrasive nature, anyway. Easy way out for everyone."

"I bet you thought again when you saw the massacre pictures. I took a glance at them and wondered about sending that to a team in Otherwhere. I counted on your new augments to keep you sane."

"Well...that worked for Toni and me." Andrew gestured to Morissa. "Our civilian passenger had her moments, but she soldiered through. Working into the team fine."

"I'm glad to hear that. Pleased you could come, Dr. Goodall." He shook her hand. "We seem to have disturbed your happy life, but I hope you'll find the change worthwhile."

"Oh, I have no doubt of that, sir."

"Neither do I. And here's the rest of the team. Chakka, you old devil. How's the boy doing?"

The auguar nuzzled up to the ambassador for a chin scratch, then looked over his shoulder at his companion.

"And this beauty would be Queen Nzinga." The ambassador bowed slightly. "A pleasure to meet you, your Majesty."

The younger auguar's eyes opened wider, and she stepped forward, touching a nose to his offered fist. Then she turned and sat with her back to his knees, facing the rest of the crowd, her head high. Chakka flopped at her side.

The ambassador grinned. "And now we have the room organized properly for an official reception. And speaking of the team, I have someone I'd like you to meet."

"Oh?"

"Yes. The situation with the barwolves requires added resources. You're never going to get anything done if you're always watching your backs. So, I'm allocating someone to watch them for you."

Andrew shot Toni a glance, so she answered. "Sounds good, sir. In what way?"

"You can hash out the details between you. I've requisitioned three of Captain Worthing's rocketjets. The Martins have already proved their ability to function in the Tree Planet's atmosphere." He grinned. "In fact, Master Pilot Jaeger speaks very highly of their maneuverability."

"He should know. He matched up to three of them with *NightHawk's* shuttle. This sounds good. S & S resources?"

"You already have a full hangar of ground support, but we'll boost the maintenance level from our naval assets. I'm also sending two new STOL Harrier 93's. They'll be primarily for fast reaction to emergencies, mostly for crew evac. We also have a Sikorsky S-82 Skycrane helicopter that was tucked away in a corner of the *Unicorn*. First evidence we found that SolarCorp had designs downplanet. Anyway, it will be available at your main base, should another retrieval be required."

Andrew exchanged glances with Toni. "I'm sure that will speed up our recon immensely. Are we getting any more shuttles?"

"Another pair. With four shuttles on sweep and *Diablo* available, you should be able to make better time with your research."

"Yes, sir. Thanks a lot."

The Admiral smiled and gestured towards the doorway, where a young woman in uniform was entering. She was similar to Morissa: tall and blonde with fine features, but she carried herself with the assurance of a model on the runway, and the way she wore her uniform made it look stylish. "And now I'd like to introduce Flight Lieutenant Alison Rowell, who will be heading the Space Arm contingent. The Lieutenant will pilot the lead Harrier and liaise with your team. Alison, this is Dr. Morissa Goodall, Science Coordinator of the expedition, Commando Lieutenant Toni Jacobs of the Feline Augment Corps, in charge of on-ground security and subject interaction. I believe you've met Andrew Collingwood, who is an ensign in the Space Arm sometimes, chief scientist on the expedition at others, and also representative to one of the major funding organizations for the project."

While he rattled on, Toni kept a pleasant smile on her fact, but her augment was busy.

NightHawk?

Aye, ma'am.

Alison Rowell. Any connection to an acquaintance of ours?

His daugher.

Thank you, NightHawk.

Completely unfazed by the cascade of new data, the Flight Lieutenant snapped a perfect salute, which Andrew and Toni returned. Then she smiled graciously and held out a hand to each of them. Her palm was dry and her grip firm but not aggressive.

"So pleased to meet you all. I'm really looking forward to this project. It's one thing to take all this training, but another to actually get boots on the ground and be useful."

91

Toni contrived to be the last to shake hands. "And here is another team member you'll want to get to know. This is Nzinka, my auguar. She handles the point in any contacts with the barwolves. Don't make the mistake of think…"

The woman wasn't really listening. Her eyes widened and her hand came out. "Oh, isn't she cu…"

Her voice cut off with a squawk as her hand was pinned between needled fangs.

Nzinka, be polite!

Emotion: disdain.

Everyone in the room froze. Alison's eyes widened further, but she knew better than to pull back.

Nzinka tightened her jaws ever so slightly, then slowly opened her mouth, her eyes staring into those of her victim.

Toni waited until the woman dropped her gaze. "She's rather particular about who touches her."

Emotion: hilarity.

Emotion: anger. Andrew Collingwood, you stay out of this!

Aye, Lieutenant. She's all yours.

"She's also very careful with humans. You were smart not to move."

The lieutenant checked over her hand, where the white points were turning red. She looked at the auguar with new respect. "She has amazing control."

"There was never any intention to hurt you. Just put you in your place."

The cool blue eyes turned directly to Toni. "And just where is that?"

"Hard to say. With auguars, it's complicated, and with Nzinga it's moreso because she's Prime of her cadre." She shrugged and grinned. "We manage. Here in the Outback the chain of command isn't quite so clear, as you can see. Do you know anything about Social Anthropology?"

"A couple of courses at university."

"We function more like the old North American Indians. The leader in any endeavour is the one with the most experience in that field. General policy is set through cooperative discussion."

Alison shot a frown towards the ambassador, but he merely smiled.

"Well." She took a closer look at each of them. "Well, here we are. I suppose we'll figure things out. Dr. Pretoro speaks very highly of all of you, and Lieutenant Jacobs, your military record is quite stellar."

She frowned down at Nzinga. "You," she pointed a finger, "and I will have words at a later date. Enough mistakes have been made. There will be no more."

Emotion: cautious acceptance.

Good girl.

Andrew cleared his throat. "Um...personal question which is more important than you might think. What level of augment do you have?"

"Standard Level nine point three with flight auxiliaries. Why is that important?"

The ambassador raised a hand. "Please, this is becoming a briefing. Let's sit down at the table and I'll have refreshments brought in."

They took their seats, Pretoro at the head. Andrew gestured Morissa to sit, then took the chair opposite her, leaving the two Lieutenants to face each other.

Rowell leaned her forearms on the edge of the table and regarded Andrew.

He nodded in response. "As I'm sure you know, the barwolves are being investigated because they have some kind of communication system similar to our augments. But their messages do not show up on mechanical receptors. The higher-level, latest-design Space Arm augments have a larger organic component, allowing those officers some level of communication with the barwolves. So your nine point three may prove to be an advantage to you in an emergency.

"Nzinga is a new development in the feline augment field, with full organics. I have had completely organic augments for ten years, and Toni has recently developed an organic system. That's why we're involved in this program."

He grinned. "It's also the topic of my thesis, so I'm doubly involved."

The Space Arm officer nodded. "I'm getting the picture." Once again, she took the time to make eye contact with each person around the table."

Andrew regarded this with a quizzical frown. *What's she doing?*

You've seen Nzinga with strangers. She's looking for weakness.

Has she tried your augment yet?

Not without permission. She's not that stupid. Her position is much too delicate to make another mistake.

Emotion: chuckle. Yes, if she needs two hands to fly her Harrier.

10.   CONFRONTATION

The meeting rambled on in a semi-formal mode, and finally everyone got up to leave. Toni motioned the other lieutenant to stay.

When the others were gone, Rowel met her eyes. "Yes, Lieutenant?

"A couple of things we need to get straight. First is chain of command. We're both the same pay grade with different specialties. As we were discussing earlier, when there's flying to be done, it's all yours. Security and dealing with the barwolves is my baliwick. That okay with you?"

"I have no problem with that. The second thing? My name, I suppose?"

"Has to be discussed. We have already had contact from your father showing interest in this project. It is too much coincidence to expect the appearance of his daughter on site to be luck."

"I can see how you might think that."

"It is unfortunate. We are a small team in a large system, and any possible source of tension or conflict between the members of the team can be fatal."

The blonde woman frowned, raising her head. "You surely can't believe that the fact of my parentage is enough to cause discord in the team."

Toni shrugged. "It's not just your parentage. It's the possibility that your father and his supporters have used their influence to get you promoted to this position and sent here, for what purposes we have no idea."

"Are you insinuating that I got my position here through the influence of my father?" The long, fine hands corded with the ferocity of her grip on the edge of the table.

Toni waited until the other woman's shoulders began to relax. "I'm quite willing to believe you are capable of filling the position you have been given. But your motives will always be suspect because of your father's position. Paternalism is a two-edged sword, I'm sure you have found before this."

"Just as your motives are suspect because of your association with Factory 4-80."

"My motives are not suspect because they are overt and clearly stated. Anyone who thinks that a spacer's complete and unthinking loyalty is to Space Arm has not read the Rules of Engagement or understood the modern military. Spacers are taught to think for themselves and hold to their own ethos. You can't be one person in your head and another person in your job or sooner or later you're going to trip yourself up. The old armies tried to brainwash their soldiers into all being the same person. It just messed them up."

"Fine. Then I could, by your argument, be a loyal Space Arm member and a supporter of an interplanetary corporation."

"You could, but you'd be in a very delicate position. One of Space Arm's main duties is to oversee and control the actions of the interplanetaries, and some day you would quite possibly be required to oversee your own group, which would be a conflict of interest, and you would be expected to excuse yourself from the situation immediately."

Toni raised a cautionary finger. "The real problem comes when your beliefs lead you to think that you are doing the best for everyone by working to aid your interplanetary masters from inside the Space Arm. At that point you become a spy."

Red crawled up the pale cheeks. "Are you accusing me of being a spy?"

"Of course not. I have no evidence. I'm only pointing out that because of the evidence I do have, I must consider the possibility that your loyalties are not wholly directed towards the Planetary Community you have sworn to protect. So, I must be careful in dealing with you."

"I see." Alison laced her fingers together and snapped her thumbnails against each other, back and forth. "At least you're being honest with me."

Toni leaned forward to demand eye contact. "I take exception to the 'at least' part of that. I am being honest with you. That is one of the most important actions I could take. Honesty builds trust. It takes a while, but it works. If you look at the group of people who have been out here the longest – O'Rourke and her crew, Pretoro, Andrew – we each have different personal objectives and desires, but we would all trust each other with our lives. That is a power impossible to buy, force, or bargain with."

She sat back. "When you've been out here a year or so and proved yourself trustworthy, you may join that group or create a group of your own. Destroy that trust and you will become one of the loneliest humans in this galaxy."

The Flight Lieutenant, too relaxed. "Hmm." She gave a small smile. "Not much to be said after that."

Toni answered the smile. "Sorry. End of sermon."

Smell: deaf/blind lady. Image: Morissa outside doorway, silent.

Thank you, Nzinga. Let her stay there.

"You really believe all that, don't you?"

"What, you think I went through all that emotion to con you?"

"Some people would."

"Then here's some more honesty. I've got you pegged as a soloist. You've been taught all your life that your own personal advancement is the one most important thing in your existence. I can't argue with that. A lot of people believe the same way. Most of the people higher up in the business world wouldn't be there if they didn't think like that.

"But that attitude doesn't function so well in the Space Arm. Yes, it can move you up the command ladder. But that kind of advancement doesn't stand you in good stead when the ordnance starts to fly. We survive and succeed as a group.

"Do you remember the old US Marine Corps movies? "No man left behind." Now, that's a dumb motto. The mission could go down the tubes and the whole troop get wiped out because they stayed to get that one man out.

"But in the long run, that organization had a high degree of success in their missions, and it was exactly because of that attitude. Unqualified support from your teammates. It can do wonders."

"You're saying that I worked my way up to my present position by using the same technniques an executive uses to fight his way up the corporate ladder, and that hasn't trained me to fulfill the duties of that role."

Toni spread her hands above the table top. "I have no idea. Before today, I didn't know that you even existed. I have never seen you give an order or interact with a subordinate. I am telling you factors I will be considering in dealing with you."

"Well, you've certainly thrown down the gauntlet. I'll take what you said into consideration."

"There you go. That expression. What does it tell me about you?"

"Throwing down the gauntlet? That's just an old expression."

"Which originally meant...?"

"A challenge..."

"...to a duel. A competition to the death."

"Don't be ridiculous. I didn't mean that!"

"Of course you didn't. But you used the expression."

The other woman looked at her. "You're going to be hard to get along with, aren't you?"

Toni smiled. "If you check my career record, you'll find quite the opposite. I'm very easy to get along with." She hunched forward and leaned her elbows on the table. "Look at it this way. I'm the nice one in this outfit. You play any games with Captain O'Rourke or Ambassador Pretoro, and you will find yourself on the next ship home before you say another word. And if you play games with Andrew...well, let's just say that nobody on *NightHawk* will play poker with him."

"You know, I think you honestly believe all that."

Toni shrugged. "That's me. Honest."

"Then let's leave it there. I have been warned, and I take the warning in the manner it was intended."

"Then we have communication, and that's the first step."

The taller woman rose and held out a hand. They shook.

"Do you really have a bronze in wrestling in the Humanorm Olympics?"

"Everybody seems to think so. Does it make a difference?"

"It speaks to your credibility."

"It speaks to my ability to visit violence on my enemies and the enemies of my friends. That's all. It has had very little effect on my life recently. Well, maybe once."

"You'll have to tell me about it some time."

"Sorry. Classified...no, really, it was part of a mission."

"I believe you."

"Oh. Good." She stood and watched the pilot walk away, graceful poise undisturbed by the recent confrontation.

Toni shook her head and was about to follow.

Emotion: warning. Deaf/blind lady is still there.

She glanced down at Nzinga, who was in the "alert" pose, her eyes on the doorway.

Toni waited. No one appeared.

Odor: deaf/blind lady.

Thank you, Nzinga. You may relax.

"Morissa, you might as well come in."

The scientist appeared in the doorway, hesitating.

Toni regarded her. "What is it? Is something wrong?"

The other woman moved into the room, gazing around. Then her eyes met Toni's. "I...wasn't sure I should intrude."

"You're not intruding. Come on in. Did you want to talk to me?"

"...I'm not sure..."

Toni relaxed into a chair, putting one boot up on the next seat. She smiled. "You already said that. You want to talk. Siddown and chat."

Morissa's posture relaxed, and she took a chair opposite. She folded her hands on the table, staring at them.

Toni waited.

Finally, her companion met her eyes. "I don't like to admit it, but I was eavesdropping."

"I know."

A frown. "You do?"

"Nzinga knew you were there. Did you hear anything you shouldn't have?"

The other woman rolled her shoulders. "Probably not. But I did learn something."

"I suppose that's progress."

"I learned what you're like when you're not being nice."

"Ah. You might find that difficult. Is there a problem?"

"I don't think I like you when you're not nice."

"When I'm not being nice, I don't worry about what people think. I have other objectives."

The scientist nodded. "And your objective with Flight Lieutenant Rowel was…?"

"Is the answer to that important to the achievement of your duty?"

"No, no…well, maybe."

Toni sat up and leaned her elbows on the table. "Morissa, this whole conversation is going nowhere. You've got a spider in your suit. Out with it."

Her companion screwed up her face. "I'm having trouble getting it all straight. You were a completely different person just now. What happened to the woman I got to know on *Diablo?* The one who spent the trip sparring with Andrew like another teenager."

"Do you know what my teenage years were like? I was small, flat-chested, and totally focused on my athletics."

A slow smile crossed the other's face. "Sounds familiar."

"You understand. So, I missed something."

Morissa sat back, her shoulders relaxing. "Ah. I see. And now…"

She swept a hand towards the doorway. "And now I have Andrew. He's smart, he's handsome, and he looks up to me. He thinks I'm sexy. Yes, I know that's hard to believe, but…oh. Okay, maybe not for you." She sat straighter. "So sometimes I indulge myself. It doesn't seem to do him any harm, and…well, that's the way we interact."

"Like a couple of teenagers."

"Exactly."

"Isn't that rather dangerous?"

"I'm aware of that."

The scientist nodded. "So in the future, I shouldn't expect you to be the person I learned to trust on the trip out here."

Toni shrugged. "You can still trust me. I am who I am. I'm not going to change how I act with you.

"You aren't? I thought, 'The holiday is over. We're on the job now, and the next time I meet Toni she's going to be cold and hard and…' well, I'm not sure I'm ready to deal with that."

Toni took a moment to understand, then produce an unforced smile. "Not going to happen. What you just saw was two alpha females sparring for Prime of the pride. You and I have our priorities straight."

"We do?"

"We do. Our primary objective is to get your research done. I'm completely under your orders until danger threatens. Then I'm the boss."

"Oh. I never looked at it that way. Yes, I suppose that's best, isn't it?"

"If we want to get this job done and both be alive at the end of it, that's best."

The other woman assessed her. "You know, when it comes right down to it, you're the Prime of this pride, aren't you? It doesn't matter who has what rank."

"Until Andrew or his mother enters the picture, that's how it is." She grinned. "You're in the jungle now, sister, and you better learn to follow the rules."

Morissa nodded. "I couldn't be in better hands."

Toni held out a fist, and the other woman, after a brief hesitation, carefully bumped it with her own. The commando grinned.

"I'm glad we got this straight. We're off to the Tree Planet in a couple of days. Once we get out there we don't know what will happen, and we have to be ready for anything. The more solid the group is before we get there, the sooner we come up to speed in response."

11. PARADISE

Ten days later *Diablo,* leading a formation of five fighters, came out of decel above the Tree Planet and began her landing orbits. The planetary system spread out below them: the main orb beautiful in its Earth-like greens and blues, the heavy rings glowing in the light of Barnard's Star. Several planetoids and moonlets swept their courses through the rubble, defining the rings with bands of empty space. Soon they were closing in on Barwolf Base, a green island in a deep blue ocean.

"Well, there it is. Home, sweet home for the next few weeks. Or months, or years. Who knows?"

Morissa gazed at the viewscreen as they neared landing. "Can we hold it here for a moment?"

Andrew grinned. "You can replay it any time you want."

"But it's not the same when you know it's down there, re-ti."

"Hovering takes more fuel. I'll deduct it from your end-of-the-month paycheque."

She grinned. "You do that."

Toni watched this interaction with her own internal grin.

Image: Andrew spinning tiny Morissa on the tips of his fingers.

Image: Morissa flat on deck, Nzinga sitting on her head.

You be a good girl. She is a pride member.

Image: Nzinga, queen of the pride.

Image: Pride Leader standing over all.

Concept: complex ideas intertwined: question, obvious answer, life, universe, acceptance.

Um...yes, that's about it, all right.

Emotion: satisfaction.

"You've got a strange look on your face, Toni." Andrew grinned. "Something bite you?"

"Yeah. Nzinga just hit me with something I've never heard from her before."

"Oh? Something interesting?"

"To your research, maybe. She and I were just tossing silliness around about people's positions in the gestalt. I reminded her at the end that I was the Pride Leader, and she better not forget it. She responded with a series of images, ideas and emotions, quite distinctly telling me that life was unfolding exactly as it should, and she was very satisfied with the way things were and why would I even bother to mention it?"

"She said all that?"

Toni shrugged. "You know how a picture is worth a thousand words. She just flashed me all those things in about two seconds."

Andrew reached down and Nzinga arched her head up for an ear scratch. *And where do I fit in this universe of yours?*

Image: auguar in rainstorm with huge drops hitting from all directions. Auguar shakes her coat dry and walks away.

Toni laughed out loud, then glanced at Morissa, who was staring at her. "Sorry, I'll never be able to explain that one. Nzinga just told Andrew in no uncertain terms not to ask stupid questions that are impossible to answer."

"I thought she only communicated in images and emotions."

"She does. That's what makes it so funny. Have you ever looked at one of those weird twentieth-century blobs they called paintings, and actually got an idea what the artist was getting at?"

"Rarely, but yes, I have."

"It's rather like that. A montage of images and emotions that makes up a message greater than the sum of its parts."

"She's learned to make a gestalt in your gestalt. Why am I not surprised?"

Toni nodded. "It might be their next stage of development. What do you think, Andrew?"

"I would love to draw certain conclusions I'm being very careful not to jump to, because I have a real scientist standing beside me. But it's certainly interesting, and we'll follow up for sure. Now can we land this thing and get on with work?"

Toni gave him a polite bow and a "go ahead" flourish of the wrist.

The viewscreens tilted as *Diablo* swooped lower, coming in over the ocean across reef-strewn shallows to a tree-lined beach. The landing field lay a few hundred metres inland, sheltered from the constant sea winds by a sweep of forest. A great shelf of rock jutted horizontally from the side of the mountain, affording a dust-free landing spot. The camp stood on the lee side of the rock, fronting a small meadow.

"Very pretty. Moderately defendable." Toni peered closer. "Doubly protected from the west. Are there strong winds?"

Andrew pulled up a climate map on the portside viewer. "This planet doesn't seem to do hurricanes, but it's a flat island with a thousand klicks of open water upwind of it, so we're being careful."

There was a lurch, and the engines began to spool down.

He grinned at their surprised faces. "I delayed the video because we were discussing it. Sorry about that."

"Not much, you aren't. Just one of your usual tricks for keeping everybody off balance. Ha. Ha."

He glanced at her, then at Nzinga. "Both of you now waxing metaphoric. Should I be concerned?"

"No, it's just the beauty of the setting and the knowledge that there aren't any barwolves around to tear us to shreds."

"Well, the nearest pack is on the mainland, thirty klicks east. But it's downwind. What if they smell us? Can they swim?"

She shrugged. "Until we get evidence that they have a sense of smell, it's going to be hard to get in a lather about it. May we deplane, boss?"

The airlock swung open and the stairs unfolded. "Please, ladies. Welcome to my version of paradise."

12.   POACHERS

They wandered away from the ship, gazing around. It was a beautiful spot, surrounded by tall, fan-boughed trees. The ground at their feet was spongy with something like moss, with small plants scattered around in bunches. A semicircle of one-story prefabs backed into the angle of the landing pad rock and the forest, with the shops and machinery upwind across the pad a good hundred metres.

Half a dozen men in fatigues sauntered over, saluted and began to offload the luggage from the hatch *Diablo* had opened. They slung the bags over their shoulders and toted them off to the camp.

"No baggage carts?"

Andrew shook his head. "No wheels on the grass. We don't know how tough the ground cover is yet." His head went up. "Here comes our escort fleet."

The three rocketjets dropped straight down and landed on their tails. The Harriers came in upwind like landing birds and feathered their engines to settle gently on the rock. Soon the five pilots were strolling towards the rest of the crew, gazing around in appreciation.

The lean, graceful figure in the lead pulled off her helmet, shaking out her shoulder-length blonde hair. "I'm looking around for hula girls and ukeleles." Her wingman, Flight Sergeant Achmed Gamal, looked puzzled.

Andrew grinned. "We're showing the 2035 version of "South Pacific" in the mess hall after dinner. All will become clear."

Morissa scoffed. "That one was directed by a gay guy. All the bare chests are men."

There was a brief silence while the newcomers digested this comment, and then the group moved towards the camp. Morissa fell into step beside Toni. "They had to know sooner or later. Better start to out on the right foot."

"You know my opinion of honesty."

106

They allowed the new crew overnight to get accustomed to the Tree Planet time zone, and then called a mid-morning assembly in the dining hall, the largest indoor space in camp.

The whole staff of the base was there: Counting the mechanics, cooks helpers, janitors, and the lot, it amounted to about 30 people, most of them military. They were under the thumb of Staff Sergeant Bob Perow, whose efficiency in the early hours of the day, they found, was only exceeded by his laxity near sunset, when he retired to his quarters to finish off the bottle he had been secretly nipping from. Unfortunately, his organizing genius extended into his drinking activities, and it proved impossible to restrict his access to the stronger forms of liquid refreshment.

Andrew surveyed the group. "Nice to see some new faces. This will add to the social variety of the camp and provide fresh input to the Saturday night poker game." Chuckles, some of anticipation, rose and faded.

"However, this will not affect our operations. We'll be running the shuttles in pairs, so that's only two sets to supervise. The rocket-jets will be on duty at all times in the research areas. The Harriers will be used for reconnaissance and emergency rescue. *Diablo* will be out and about, transporting Dr. Goodall for her special projects and whatever is required. Debriefings as usual at nineteen hundred hours. Any questions?"

One of the shuttle pilots raised a hand. "What's the official position relative to the massacre?"

Andrew nodded to Morissa, who stood.

"Our main objective, as you all know, is to collect our data without interfering with the society we are observing. There isn't much doubt that somehow we caused or influenced the massacre, which skewed the data in that area and rendered it useless. Besides creating the deaths of seventy of our subjects.

"So, our motivation is doubled. We must try twice as hard not to be observed and to protect our own people. Otherwise, business as usual."

Andrew glanced at the Staff Sergeant, then at Toni, who shook her head. The man was too relaxed to make a statement.

She stood. "Analysis of the damaged shuttle indicated a leaking hydraulic seal that would have been rectified in the next monthly maintenance. Simply bad luck that it jumped the gun, and no reflection on Master Sergeant Jasperson and his mechanics."

Jasperson stood. "Those seals have been inspected on all shuttles. No sign of more trouble, but we replaced them all."

Andrew waited, but there were no more questions. "All right. Tomorrow's a new rotation. Let's put this disturbance behind us, get back in the groove and get this job done."

He turned away, and the crew rose and began to move about their business. His glance invited Toni, Morissa and Alison, and they followed him to the small semi-private corner that was all the base could provide by way of an officer's lounge. There he stepped behind the bar and poured each of them her usual drink, cracking a cola for himself.

"Well, what do you think?"

Morissa sipped her drink. "You had a decent crew before. If we new Charlies can fit in, we'll keep the ball rolling."

"You've been through this before?"

She smiled. "Jungle and desert camps are the life of an anthropologist of any sort. It's not often you get one in a temperate climate like this. No bugs, no diseases, no natives or large predators. In other words, nothing to keep us from getting our work done in an efficient scientific manner, so we can depend on our data and make our report with all confidence that our conclusions are the correct ones."

Andrew and Toni grinned at each other. "Sounds good."

Rowell knocked back her drink and pushed the glass forward for a refill. "Here's a toast to an entertaining but not too exciting tour of duty."

They all drank.

* * *

A week of routine patrols left them all feeling quite satisfied with themselves. The barwolves were settled down, going about their lives in what were becoming very predictable ways as the scientists amassed data.

The disturbance to their happy routine came in a call from Captain O'Rourke.

"Andrew, could you get the department heads together, please? Change of plans."

When they were all gathered around the large viewscreen in the mess, Natalia started.

"I don't know if you have noticed, but we have been running another project on your planet."

Staff Sergeant Perow nodded. "We caught glimpses several times, but since they all had Space Arm FOF transponders and they stayed clear of our research areas, we ignored them."

"The pilots were told not to disturb your subjects or your studies. Well, we've gathered their data, and the conclusions are disturbing."

Toni frowned. "Security-wise, ma'am?"

"It's almost certain that someone has been picking up barwolves and taking them offplanet. Worse than that, we think they've been doing it for some time."

Morissa was on her feet. "How long? How many? Do you think the barwolves are aware of the kidnapping?"

"We're beginning to reassess that hunting expedition Andrew and Toni disturbed two years ago. It could very well be they were not sport hunting, but collecting food for their research subjects. Several unexplained pieces of equipment noted in *Diablo's* video record now look a whole lot like traps. In other words, they wouldn't have shot those barwolves. They were probably going to capture a few."

Morissa jolted upright. "They have been testing this species already for two years?"

"It is possible."

Andrew nodded slowly. "It would explain the attack on our shuttle. If the barwolves got word that shuttles were stealing their pack members…"

"That definitely fits, if the barwolves have a method of communicating that sort of information."

"Do you know where they are keeping them?"

Natalia indicated the map. "Arborea has its own complicated orbital system, with a small asteroid belt and several moonlets. Fortunately, we took a course observation on our hunting and gathering friends and were able to back-date the trajectories of the orbiters. We used that data to narrow down our observations, and we finally tagged one of their capture ships. They were headed for a small moon about half-way out the asteroid belt. Spheroid, a thousand klicks in diameter. We have scouted nearby without risking a close approach, and there are definite marks of multiple takeoffs and landings, but no structures visible."

"An underground lab?"

"Our best guess."

Morissa frowned and stared at the viewscreen. "Why haven't we been informed long before this?"

Natalia shook her head. "Space Arm security protocols, fragmentation of effort and plain old bureaucracy. Plus the fact that it made no difference to your research, and you couldn't do anything about it anyway. You're not a police force."

Toni cocked her head to one side. "But you're telling us now because…?"

"Because over the last two months they've stepped up their activities. They may have kidnapped as many as forty barwolves. With the evidence from the massacre, we are now concerned that their so-called research will either backfire or result in a much more serious problem. Plus, you are now better suited to handle the situation. *Diablo* can scout around, the Harriers and Martins can provide backup if needed. Chase this problem down and report in. Don't take any action unless it's absolutely necessary. Do you understand me, Andrew?"

"I'm afraid I do, ma'am." He met Toni's eyes and grimaced.

"Well, there you have it. If *NightHawk* was anywhere in the vicinity we'd come give you a hand, but we aren't, and we're not going to be. You've got as good a team as we could put together, and Ambassador Pretoro and I have full confidence in you. "

13.   GOD OF CUBS

After O'Rourke signed off, they held a brief meeting. Over Flight Lieutenant Rowell's protests, Andrew decided to make a preliminary expedition with only *Diablo*.

Toni backed him up. "We've been here before, Alison. It's a big mistake to go rushing off after a red herring, leaving our main mission unguarded. You and Achmed and the Martins keep doing your usual patrols. Now that we know there are nasties in the vicinity, that's even more important. I would suggest that if you catch them in the act, you force them down and arrest them for breaking the quarantine. Now that we know where their lab is, we don't need to give them free rein. What do you think, Andrew?"

"I'm glad you said that, because that means it isn't just me wanting revenge. Alison, you guys need to stay here and protect our subjects. Besides, if we're nosing around their base, we don't want one of their ships showing up unannounced to drop off a fresh catch of barwolves."

Morissa nodded. "My vote would be to keep protecting my clients. I'm sorry about the kidnap victims, and it sounds cruel, but they're already contaminated by their experience, and if they are returned they could skew our results."

Toni raised her eyebrows at the pilot. "That all right with you?"

Rowell nodded. "It's logical. But don't overextend yourselves. If you need help, give us a call. I calculate ten hours to get there."

The Science Coordinator mused a moment. "I think I'd better come along with you, though. In the second stage of the project we need to find out how barwolves get along with humans, and this group constitutes a ready-made sample."

Andrew rose. "All right. *Diablo* lifts in one hour. We don't need to attach our fuel tank for that short hop, so we can be there in about seven hours. The rest of you stick to your usual schedules, except the fighters need to expand their coverage. Push your velocity a bit. It's worth the extra fuel."

"Right, and we can fly higher, because we know we're looking for a shuttle."

Toni was already moving. "There's some gear I need to load."

* * *

Eight hours later they were under full stealth in the shelter of a gathering of minor asteroids, coasting towards the target moonlet. They soon identified the landing site, blasted clean of dust and gravel. They took a wide circle and came in from the opposite side of the planetoid, setting down ever so gently and staying quiet.

From their position just below the horizon *NightHawk* could get a multi-sensor image of the base. The working and living area was one level below ground with what looked like storage and machinery on the next level down.

Nzinga, we need a picture of their systems.

Image: schematic of base's circuitry, main floor.

What they hadn't counted on was the high level of augment activity.

Diablo, overlay that with sonic, radar, and infrared. Something's going on down there, and I want to know what it is.

What started as a scattering of different augment voices like babble in a crowded room began to solidify into a single entity. Soon there was one huge presence, vague but powerful, and definitely upset.

Emotion: frustration, fear, pain, anger!

Images: heat signatures moving towards containment laboratory. Blast doors closing.

Emotions: calming, calming, sleeping.

"They've gassed them."

"A good way to control them."

"I wonder how often that happens? Have we triggered their defenses?"

Andrew raised a finger. *Nzinga, will you do a job for me?*

Emotion: eager agreement.

Help me take a stroll. Image: Base security systems.

Toni followed to the best of her ability as the two plunged into the software, tracing the paths towards their goal.

There we have it. Security records. Let's do a quick scan

Images: security cameras scrolling rapidly through the day's events, moving backwards.

"There...and there again...oh, twice in one hour that time...Good enough."

They pulled their minds back to the ship.

"Well done, Nzinga. They've had to gas the barwolves five times in the past three days, so I doubt if this incident triggered anything. The new influx of minds must have reached some overload point, and they're in trouble down there."

"Okay, so now we plan."

"Right. But first we have to put Morissa in the picture."

"That would be useful."

Andrew ran through the situation quickly, then looked at the scientist. "If we wanted to decommission this hive mind, how would we go about it?"

She shook her head. "Nothing in our data so far gives any clue. The only thing we have statistics for is that twenty is a safe number." She thought a moment. "Twenty family or clan members. We don't know about strangers."

"We can't get a good count, but I'd say they have almost fifty there."

"Gestalt is your field, but I'd say we need to take a bunch away to calm things down."

"We might be able to pull a group of, say, fifteen out at once?"

"Are you thinking of putting them in here?" She looked around the tiny lounge.

"Even better, we put ten in here, one in each cabin, and two in the bridge."

Toni shook her head. "No, two in each cabin, and we lock the bridge hatch. Any trouble, and we gas the lot."

"Good idea. So we're looking to bust fifteen of them loose. Ideas?"

"Don't even bother with the gestalt." Toni snapped her sidearm back into its holster. "Somebody has to go in there and be hands for that pack. Once the cage doors are open, they can take care of themselves. Obviously that somebody has to be me."

Andrew clouted Toni's shoulder. "Good plan. And now may we use the gestalt to make it as safe as we can?"

"Of course."

"And you have to take Nzinga."

"I don't think so."

"Yes, you do. She's the only chance you have to control the barwolves once they're free. Remember, we haven't absolutely proven that the trigger is numbers. They did attack that shuttle, and we only think we know why."

"So Nzinga selects one sample. We turn it free. She directs it out of the room. If it obeys, we let the others go as quickly as it seems safe."

"Sounds good."

"What are we going to do with the staff?" Andrew re-accessed the gestalt. "By the electronics they're associated with, I'd say there's four scientists in the lab plus five others. Best guess is a cook, a maintenance engineer and three security. Two of them seem to be off duty, so it's not certain."

Toni thought a while. "Lock them up. I can come in with Nzinga, and she'll know where everyone is. I just sweep through, lock them in where I find them. Then I bring the barwolves out. You can set *Diablo* down against the main lock and troop them in."

"And if something goes wrong?"

"Then we blow the main lock, jam *Diablo* hard against it, and fish the barwolves in as they blow out the door."

"You're serious?"

She grinned. "Probably the only part of the whole action I've actually practised. Standard Commando training. You wanna see the manual?"

"Yes, I'll look it over. The top of the main hatch is clear of obstructions. I'm sure I can bring *Diablo* down against it."

Toni nodded. "All right. Let's get into the gestalt and fine-tune this operation. Morissa, we'll keep an image up on the visual display so you can follow."

"Thanks. I feel rather useless."

"You get the 'outside observer' role. Dr. Pretoro plays it for us sometimes. I'll explain later."

They dove into the planning, running probabilities and simulations, trying to predict what the base crew would do, what the barwolves might do, and a hundred other variables. When they finally had it polished. They ran through a dozen full simulations on VR.

Afterwards, they sat around the table with hot drinks, each with his or her own thoughts. Finally, Andrew broke the silence. "Well, Morissa, any thoughts from your point of view?"

She shrugged. "Thinking 'up and out,' what happens if a shuttle shows up in the middle of this?"

"Good point. We'll scan nearby space before we start. We should take another tour of the whole moon as well, to make sure this really is a solo habitation."

"If everything goes well, the barwolves will probably behave as planned. If Toni gets into a firefight with security, they might go wild. What do we do then?"

"Toni?"

"Assuming I win the firefight, I let them out one at a time. Nzinga escorts them one at a time, assuming that she can handle them. Toni felt anger burning in her. "If there's a firefight, I won't be leaving any humans around who could be dangerous."

"I won't tell you how to do your duty. I'm just reminding you that this is not a Commando raid, and Nzinga is not a defenseless cub."

"Got that, sir. I'm aware of my limitations."

"Good enough. Any other comments...?"

"Inbound vessel, sir. Friendly."

"Who?"

"Lieutenant Rowell."

"Is she coming in straight?"

"No, she's keeping under whatever cover she can."

"Contact her, please, Diablo."

"Harrier Romeo 1, this is Diablo calling. R-1, Diablo calling."

"Hello, Diablo. Rowell here. Permission to join you."

Andrew flipped the com open. "Heads up for other vessels and stay below the horizon on the lab please, Lieutenant. Meeting point is antipodal to the lab."

"Roger that, Mr. Collingwood."

"Will you do us a favour and sweep the planetoid for human artifacts as you come in?"

"Can do. See you in ten minutes at these coordinates."

"*Diablo* out."

"Rowell out."

Diablo, take us to those coordinates. Sweep for man-made artifacts as we go.

Lifting now, sir. Full stealth.

He regarded his companions. "What does she want here?"

Toni frowned. "If she's just coming to help, it's no problem. If she has other objectives..."

"...then it's a big problem. You still don't trust her?"

She shrugged one shoulder. "I have no evidence, just undeserved suspicion."

"And your finely-honed sense of preservation is what's keeping us alive. What are the possibilities?"

"First, she's collecting information for her father, and she's just snooping. Second, she's an active agent, here to stop our mission. Third, she's really here to help."

"Is this mission or this base important enough to blow her cover?"

"I can't see it."

Andrew nodded. "Then we assume the best and prepare for the middle worst. Nobody told her specifically not to come, so as long as her patrols are covered we can't complain. She is in charge of her unit. Is there any sense in hiding anything from her?"

"We don't have to give her the details. We're rescuing as many barwolves as we can handle, keeping the number below detonation threshold."

"Fair enough. Morissa?"

"Intrigue is not my specialty, Andrew. Whatever you wish."

"Good enough. Let's see what she says. It wouldn't hurt to have a Harrier standing off a kilometre or two minding our backs."

Soon airlocks hissed and the lanky figure of the Lieutenant jacknifed up through the doorway and stood, pulling off her helmet. She nodded to Toni and Morissa and saluted Andrew casually. "So, what's up?"

"I was about to ask you the same thing. Just passing?"

"No, I came out to investigate a suspicious silence from this area."

"A suspicious silence."

"Yes. From you. I figured you were either up to something, in which case you might want a hand, or you were in trouble, in which case it goes double. But mainly is was playing taxi driver." She turned to the airlock.

A larger figure appeared with equal agility, bouncing to attention with his helmet under his arm. "Sergeant Jackson reporting for duty, ma'am."

118

The former guard managed to get in a salute before Toni jumped up and grabbed him around the neck, the only part she could attack. "Jackson! What the hell are you doing out here?"

When she let him go, he began to remove his suit. "Nice to see you, too, Toni. I'm spying for the ambassador, I guess. He calls it a "fact-finding mission." I gather you found what you expected?"

"A scientific lab buried in the moon's surface."

He nodded. "It's hard to hide the disturbance of multiple shuttle takeoffs in moondust."

"And inside we have about fifty barwolves in individual cages. Going rapidly bonkers, we assume. Our fear is that the scientists will have orders to destroy the whole group if they are discovered. We're thinking about grabbing about fifteen of them, but not sure what to do about the humans once we've neutralized them."

"Neutralized. What does that word mean to a Commando?" Alissa's glance slid to Toni.

"I can't see killing nine humans on the chance that they might destroy a bunch of what may or may not be regarded intelligent creatures."

Glances slid to Morissa, who shrugged. "You all know I'm leaning towards intelligence, but nothing official yet."

"Hmm. And I can't see inducing a bunch of scientists to threaten a Commando enough that she can excuse wiping them out."

"Three are security guards. I have to treat the rest as non-combatants."

"I agree." The pilot glanced around. "Assuming the barwolves are an intelligent species, what we have is a standard hostage situation with fifty captives."

"That about covers it. What do you know about hostage situations?"

"I'm a Flight Lieutenant. A pilot. This is where your original briefing back on *Unicorn* becomes clear. Lieutenant Jacobs, you have the training. You're in charge."

"Jackson?"

"Theory only, ma'am. I'll follow your lead."

"Thank you. But until hostilities arise, Andrew is still in command, unless it comes to dealing with the barwolves, in which case we look to Morissa."

All eyes turned to Andrew.

"I'm reappraising. First thing we should have done is sent for backup. Where's Achmed, Lieutenant?"

"On patrol. He'll have to fuel up before he leaves. Ten hours."

"The rocketjets?"

"They could be here in twelve. Ten if they could count on a refuel before they returned to base."

"*Diablo*, give Lieutenant Rowell radio access, please."

"*Radio access approved for Flight Lieutenant Rowell, sir.*"

"Please send to all four of them to arrive in ten hours if possible. If *Romeo 2* is hitting base, have him pick up one of the marines and...one package CC75-B19 from the far left-hand end of the green warehouse. Emergency medical supplies."

"CC75-B19. Got it."

Toni had a sudden thought. "Tell the marine to arm for on-ship action and to bring a couple of cans of Snoozo."

"Sure enough. Snoozo?"

"The commando term for a gas that does what it sounds like. If we waited until the next time they gassed the barwolves and we Snoozed the atmo system we could just walk in."

Rowel glanced back to Andrew. "That's all?"

"For now, yes. Use the left-hand couch on the bridge."

"Got it, sir." Alison ducked out the door and walked forward.

Andrew turned to Toni. "Other resources?"

"None of the shuttles could get here from Arborea inside two days. *NightHawk* is roaming the Outer Belt somewhere."

"The destroyers?"

"*Saskatchewan's* the nearest, twenty-seven hours away but headed outsystem. *Nebraska's* at the embassy: more like three days."

Andrew spread his hands. "There we have it, folks. It's all on us, in ten hours plus. From the feel of their gestalt, I don't think the barwolves can hold it together much longer than that. We'll have to rendezvous with the other ships and bring our manpower aboard. Probably better to feed and rest them first. *Diablo*, do you have a good recipe for chili?"

"*Vegetariano* or *con carne, señor?*"

"Whatever we have the most of." He grinned. "We'll have a motivated fighting force once they find out where they'll be bunking if they don't take that base."

"All right. As soon as the lieutenant is clear, I'll call up the Unicorn and have an S&S team sent out. We'll need the basics: food, medical, fuel, maybe some mechanical, though I can't think what."

Toni drew her sidearm and aimed at a dot on the far wall. "If things don't go well, there may be maintenance needed on the base."

"I suppose. Also, if this is a hostage situation, we can't just take fifteen and leave the rest. The chances are too great they'd be slaughtered the moment we pulled out."

Tony nodded. "When you put it in those terms, our old plan becomes a last-ditch tactic. If all hostages are in immediate danger of death, grab those we can and forget the rest. A hard decision to make."

"Best case, we take over the base and hold it until we can get the barwolves pulled out in an orderly manner. Not as dramatic as our original plan, but much more practical."

Toni regarded the assembled crew. "Right. So, my ground assault group is Jackson and one marine plus five pilots with various levels of combat training. Andrew, I assume you're covering the front door with *Diablo*. You'll have them aboard, ready to jump in when I need them. Lieutenant, I'm not that familiar with your Harrier. What can it do, solo, if you stay on *Diablo*?"

Rowell grimaced. "Less than it could before they Asimoved the whole fleet. It can defend itself and it can defend a position I am holding, but it can't attack a human ship if I'm not on board. To override that command it must be linked with other members of the fleet under human command. The rocketjets are programmed the same."

"Then once you come inside to help me, Andrew could coordinate all four vessels to hold our backs if trouble shows up?"

"Certainly. It's rather complicated, but..."

"We have ten hours to practice." The boy grinned. "Sounds like a good way to fill the time."

"And Nzinga and I have time for recon."

Andrew frowned. "What did you have in mind?"

"We need to get in close. You can drop us off over the horizon, which is only about a hundred metres, and we'll walk in."

"Don't you think they'll notice someone stomping around on their roof?"

"We don't need to get that close. We just want to learn their scanning system, their com tower and its capacity. From closer in we can do better exploratory work in their security systems. Nzinga and I don't have the training or experience you and Chakka have, so the best we can do is map it all and bring it back to you for analysis."

"Sounds like a plan."

"It is. First, we go into our gestalt and run some simulations. That will give me an idea what info we need. Then the Cat and I go walkabout, and when we come back, we finalize the plan."

Lieutenant Rowell appeared in the doorway. "Backup on the way. What can Morissa and I do, meanwhile?"

"If you wouldn't mind, take your ship out and make a couple more sweeps around this side of the moon, looking for anything human in origin. We don't want to find out they had a physical back door or another sensor array."

"I could conceal myself in that clump of asteroids about a hundred klicks outsystem and wait until the moon's rotation brings the base into sight, then do a passive scan of that side as well."

"Good thinking."

The pilot grinned. "Planetary survey techniques."

Andrew was watching Morissa. "And if you really want something to do, Doctor?"

"I certainly do."

"Use *Diablo's* organic augment to keep tabs on our hostages. The information will not be precise, but if you take your time and build up a picture, you can watch it change over time. You might get a better idea of numbers, and it would be very useful if we knew any schedules they keep, either the barwolves or their captors."

"May I use the bridge viewscreens?"

"By all means."

To be safe, Andrew dropped Toni and Nzinga off a kilometer from the horizon of the base. They loped the first few hundred metres, then slowed to a crawl as the radio tower became visible.

Give us a picture of the surface electronics, Nzinga.

Image: triangle of camera/radio/radar receivers sweeping the landing area and the main airlock. Manhole airlock to the east side. Ten-metre high transmission tower well clear of the landing.

That's it?

Emotion: eager desire to please.

That's all we can find, Andrew. Need anything else?

There's a flaw in their layout. If you approach the airlock from 273 degrees, the transmission tower hides you from the southeast camera for most of its sweep.

She circled the perimeter. *Heading in at 273.*

Hold it there. Waiting for the camera sweep. Move in 5...3, 2, 1, go.

Roger. She slipped in and flattened herself behind the tower with her auguar down in the shadows at its base. *This is plenty close. Nzinga, let's start with the main hatch and move down, one tier at a time.*

They scanned the electronics of the base security and physical plant, zooming in for details at Andrew's request. Toni was starting to get stiff from standing in one place when he pronounced himself satisfied.

"Let's take a look at the security office."

Nzinga inserted them into the camera on the wall overlooking the security desk. The chair in front of it was empty. Seven viewscreens showed the base going about its daily routines.

"Hey, look at that."

On the screen, two guards and a scientist were wrestling a barwolf in a cage onto a dolly, which they wheeled into an adjoining room. There they covered the cage with several different fabrics in turn, reading their instrumentation each time, frowning and recording numbers.

Doesn't look like they're having much luck.

Since they're trying to use mechanical tools to sense organic augment output, I don't think luck would help.

The lab workers gave up and wheeled the barwolf back to its fellows, sparking another scene of restlessness and pacing. But this one was different.

Andrew, what's going on?

I don't know. This isn't random panic...they're forming a gestalt on purpose this time!

Hazy image: silver beast against black sky and stars, looking down.

Holy Crap! That's Nzinga. They know she's up here.

Image: Great silver beast with barwolf cubs at his feet. Question?

That's Chakka. How do these barwolves know about Chakka? Tell her to say she isn't him.

Emotion: negative.

Emotion: question?

Image: Chakka the Warrior in space armour, standing with barwolf cubs at his feet. Queen Nzinga stands at his side.

Emotion: joyful acceptance. Emotion: great need. Longing for freedom. Longing for peace.

Emotion: sympathy.

Are you getting all this, Andrew?

I think so.

Image: shining two-legged upright being beside Queen Nzinga. Emotion: question?

Image: Chakka's cub and Pride Leader stand with Chakka and Nzinga. Emotion: pack togetherness.

Emotion: acceptance.

"*Okay, we've been accepted by the gestalt.*" Toni spoke in the com for Morissa's benefit.

Andrew did the same. "*What do we do now?*"

Emotion: longing for freedom.

Emotion: waiting

Emotion: pain, worry, fear, growing anger.

Image: barwolves pacing, gnawing at iron bars, throwing their heavy shoulders against cage doors.

Nzinga, we'd better get out of here. We're causing that.

Emotion: agreement.

Image: overlay of base's circuitry. Heat signatures moving towards containment laboratory. Blast doors closing.

Emotions: calming, calming, sleeping.

Gassed them again.

Let's get you out while they're occupied, Toni. You're out of camera range...now. Make it quick.

They bounded flat and low, diving to the moon's surface as they crossed the imaginary horizon line of the cameras. Right into a drift of moon dust.

Oops. Forgot about our dust cloud.

Nothing we can do about that. Nobody was on duty in the control room, and they've got no reason to rewind. Could be a meteorite strike.

Should we be worried about tracks?

What's the surface like?

There are lots of footprints in this area, but most are partially covered by dust from recent landings. New tracks do show, but there's quite a few of those as well.

More risk in staying to wipe them out. Come on in, team. We have what we need.

On our way.

The three sat in the bridge of *Diablo,* staring at each other. Nzinga slid over and put her head in Toni's lap for a reassuring ear-scratch.

"What now?"

He wiped his brow, which glistened with sweat. "Wowee! That was one powerful mind."

"Vague and unfocused, though."

He nodded. "That's how our gestalts always seem to me before I focus them."

"They need a catalyst."

"I guess so."

"You mean, if you were to take control of that hive mind in there, you could turn it into…"

"There's about fifty of them. Something orders of magnitude more mentally powerful than the whole *NightHawk/Diablo* gestalt."

"But still in cages down there on that moon."

"Exactly."

"I guess the question is whether we want the barwolf gestalt to stay in one piece."

"Definitely not. It would be an aberration with untold power to do good or evil. Knowing the barwolves even as little as we do…"

"Actually, I have some input on that subject. I think you should be very wary about thinking in terms of controlling their gestalt."

They both turned to Morissa.

"Why is that? I control the *NightHawk* and *Diablo* gestalts."

"Because they are set up with minds trained to a hierarchical society. What do you know about termites? Ants? Bees?"

They both stared at her.

"Let me guess. You have a picture of a hive or nest, with thousands of workers controlled by a queen at the centre."

They both nodded hesitantly.

"Completely wrong. About as accurate as looking at a human city and thinking it was run by the electrical generating plant or the hospital. In fact, the queen has nothing to do with the decision-making process. She does nothing but reproduce."

"But ant hills and beehives make all sorts of decisions."

"Right, and the model for that process is much more like the function of the human brain. It's made up of a whole bunch of units — cells or ants or bees — having interactions with each other, and the total effect is a change in behaviour of the group. I studied termites, but the same applies to all of them."

Andrew was thinking. "There is no leader. The individuals don't have the concept of obedience at all."

"If you could ask an ant, she would tell you that she was making all her decisions for herself. Because in one sense she is. Of course she's basing those decisions on inbred rules, but she doesn't know that." Morissa smiled. "Sort of like humans."

"Aha. So if the barwolves have no inbred sense of obedience and no societal behaviours that practice obedience..."

"Then we have two problems. The first is that you must be very careful about thinking you can control them, because central control is foreign to their natures. The second is that it's going to be difficult to classify their intelligence. We will probably have to redefine the term."

Andrew laughed. "Now you're starting to sound like your famous ancestor."

127

"There are similarities."

Toni had been thinking on another line. "Wait a minute. But the barwolves do have a hierarchy. When Chakka dominated them, they had a ritual that showed submission. *Diablo,* can you run that video for us?"

"This one?"

The viewscreen showed a barwolf, head turned to the side, sliding up to Chakka and touching his foreleg with one paw.

Morissa frowned in concentration. "I've seen that footage before, but not in this context. *Diablo,* can you run the whole sequence, please?"

"Aye, ma'am."

Again the first barwolf demonstrated submission, the other two following. The cubs scooted away, obeying the command of the largest creature.

Morissa nodded. "Fair enough. That partially solves the problem. But I still suggest Andrew be very careful."

"No argument from me. That's a scary being down there."

Toni nodded. "We don't dare waken them. We have to get them out of there as they are. Once they are separated, the gestalt will disappear."

"Or we destroy them."

"Andrew!"

"Do you see any other alternative?"

She shrugged miserably. "It would certainly be easy."

"Yes. Just turn them loose. They'd take care of it in no time flat."

Toni shuddered. "That's a last resort if I ever heard one."

"Agreed. But what can we do? Even at their present state they are very intelligent, but they can't do anything but think. They're like a brain in a box. They can't affect the outside world."

"They don't have to. All they have to do is persuade one human to take their part. Can you imagine a superbrain being able to persuade you that the very best thing you could possibly do is to take it onboard *Diablo?*"

Andrew leaned his elbows on the table. "Let's get into our own gestalt and do some planning. We need to have something ready when the Lieutenant gets back from her sweeps. *Diablo*, keep updating Dr. Goodall's viewscreen so she can follow as much as possible."

They spent the next two hours planning, testing, and polishing. By the time *Diablo* announced the approach of the R-1, they had it worked out.

Toni and Nzinga would penetrate the base, Jackson following. As she subdued the crew, he would secure them until she reached the lab. Jackson would hold the captives in the mess hall while Toni cleaned up. Once everyone was under control, or in case of emergency, Andrew would bring *Diablo* and connect to the main airlock. If they were discovered, Nzinga would close all the interior safety doors. Toni and the pilots would clear each section, one at a time.

Andrew gathered them all together once Alison had removed her suit.

"Here's the schedule. Toni and Nzinga, you're off-watch for the next four hours. I want you fresh as daisies for the attack. Jackson and I will spend an hour with Lieutenant Rowell, bring her up to speed and run a few simulations. Then we're off for three hours.

"That brings us to zero minus two hours. We can start feeding information to the incoming pilots, so everyone's ready to roll the moment they hit tarmac. Or moon dust, as it happens in this case. The rendezvous point is the next moonlet upspin. *Diablo* will be monitoring base activity, so we'll have more data for choosing the best time in their schedule to hit them.

"Morissa, I'd like you to sit in with the Lieutenant and me in case you come up with something appropriate. After that, your time is your own."

"Did I hear the word 'chili' mentioned?"

"You did. I have all the ingredients thawing and hydrating."

"My camp chili was renowned. I'll take care of feeding the mob."

"That would be great. *Diablo,* please set Dr. Goodall at a Level Three for kitchen security."

Lieutenant Rowell half-frowned. "You have levels of kitchen security?"

He grinned. "No, I just said that to make Morissa feel more important."

He ducked as an empty cup floated past his ear in the light gravity to bounce gently off the wall behind his head.

Toni grinned to herself. *He's doing it again. He'll have them wrapped around his fingers in no time.* Then a serious thought hit her. *I wonder if Asimov's Laws should apply to Andrew?*

14. UNDERGROUND ASSAULT

Entry into the upper airlock chamber went smoothly, with Nzinga blurring out whatever camera was pointing their way, then turning each one back on as they passed. They had chosen their entry for a time when no one manned the security desk. One of the guards was in the lounge and one was on patrol down near the south end by the labs.

The delicate point came when she had to get Nzinga and herself out of armour. Jackson had decided to leave his on in case of a real firefight. He had no particular commando training, so subtlety wasn't his forté. He stood guard while Toni tried to get the auguar out of her suit without making any noise. It wasn't working.

Andrew, we need a distraction. Can you stir up the barwolves, just a little bit?

That's like asking me to set off a bomb just a little...no, it's okay, I'll try.

Vaguely, in a corner of her mind, she could feel the pressure of the barwolf gestalt begin to build. She disregarded it and tugged Nzinga's spacesuit free. Then she slipped out of her own, and on a thought, clipped it back together and stood it behind the door from the airlock into the main base.

She grinned at Jackson. *Someone covering our backs.*

He nodded and gestured her to lead.

She gently jacked an antipersonnel round into the chamber of her assault rifle, slung it behind her shoulder, drew her sidearm and peered ahead. The gestalt VR showed the cook in the kitchen, one guard watching the viewscreen in the lounge, the engineer in his bedroom, and all four scientists in the labs. The other security guard was in the lower level, which bothered her. His only access to the lab floor was the freight elevator or up the stairs where her suit was standing. At the moment he was stationary in the Environmental Equipment room in the central area, so no trouble yet.

Keeping the picture in her mind, she slipped forward, Nzinga glued to her side.

The cook was easy. He was a tall, thin African man, singing a tribal song to himself and dancing gently as he stirred something on the stove. She touched the back of his head with her gun barrel, and he turned, his voice stopping in a startled squawk, his eyes bugging out. She put a finger to her lips and pointed to the floor. While he was getting down she turned towards the lounge, and Jackson slipped in behind her, restraints in hand.

The guard was surprised as well, and Nzinga squashed his attempt to send an augment message. She took care of this one personally, aware of how some security people were trained in escaping from any sort of restraint. When he was safely bound and gagged, she moved on.

Checking to see that no one had moved, she slipped into the bedroom hallway and easily subdued the engineer, who had no time to even get up off his bed.

Then, just as she was about to leave his room, she heard soft footsteps. The third guard was strolling along the outside corridor, headed for the kitchen area.

Alert: guard coming down the hall. Nzinga, down.

Emotion: agreement

Emotion: agreement.

All this time the barwolf gestalt was firming and growing. It pressed on her mind, a surging desire for clarity, for unity, for freedom.

Shaking her head, she waited, peering through the hinge crack of a half-open door.

The guard strolled by, not even glancing in. She listened.

Nothing.

She crept to the hall doorway and peered around.

The man's broad back moved away. Just past the kitchen doorway, he stopped.

He spotted something. Nzinga, jam his augment.

Emotion: agreement.

The guard drew his pistol and moved forward in a crouch, his weapon held in the two-handed fashion approved by most police forces.

Can you take him, Jackson?

Too far away. Shoot?

Not yet. Let's see what he does.

Suddenly the guard broke. He sprang to the right, into the loading bay. Toni sprinted silently down the hall, but she was too late. As she entered the bay the freight elevator closed, its motors whining.

Stay here, Jackson. I'll round up the scientists. Nzinga, close and lock all doors in the lower story. Can you stop the elevator?

Emotion: negative. Image: doors closing.

"Andrew, our cover is blown. Move in."

"On our way."

She turned back down the hall, reading the heat signatures in her VR. Two in the first office, two in the lab. Big windows between the areas.

No time to be subtle. I'm going in.

She burst into the office, cowed the two men sitting at their desks and whipped a quick turn of securitape around their wrists and ankles, gags around their faces. Then she shoved them to the floor and moved out.

In the lab, two younger men were assembling a piece of equipment, so intent on their task they didn't look up until her boots came into their line of vision. Their reactions would have been comical if she hadn't been in such a hurry.

"Faces to the wall. Hands behind you."

She taped their wrists, then prodded them down the hall to the lounge, where Jackson had the others sitting in a row. A brief nod to him, then she was back down the hall to collect the others.

Okay, NightHawk. We have seven subjects under control. Two security guards in the basement.

What do you plan to do with them?

If we had time, we could starve them out, I suppose.

If they didn't starve you for air, first.

Emotion: question?

The environmental equipment room. All the air feeds, water reclamation, you name it. They might even have gas. We're just approaching the airlock. Can you keep them occupied until we can get a larger force down to you?

Come on in, but I'm going down after them now.

Your call. On our way.

Once you take over the prisoners, Jackson can come down and help me pick up the pieces. By the way, you can take the pressure off the barwolves, now. They're starting to get to me.

I haven't been putting any pressure on. Maybe you should gas them.

I'd rather not. Don't worry about them. I can handle it. The guards will split up and hide in the storage area in hopes of an ambush. She scanned her VR. *They've met in the machine shop, probably for a tool to break the lock, and now they're heading for the equipment room. Gotta go. Jacobs out.*

She sprinted for the stairs, Nzinga following closely. When they reached the bottom, she looked out cautiously. *Diablo* achieved a better angle as she got above the lab, and her battle gestalt gave clearer information. At the sound of her footsteps the two guards had retreated from the equipment room and headed right where Toni had predicted, a single huge room filled with a warren of aisles of shelving. She paused outside the door. The lock had been forced.

I'm going in to flush them out. Is there anything you can do about those damn barwolves? They're putting constant pressure on me now.

What do you mean, pressure?

I don't have time to explain, but they want to join my gestalt with Nzinga. It's a real distraction, like static on a com system. Can you get them off my back?

I'll work on it.

She registered her opponents on the VR map and moved into the intersecting corridors, sending Nzinga in a flanking movement. A plan was coming together in her head, like a chess game where she could already see the end.

Then one of the guards disappeared.

Crap. He's found some kind of heat shield. This one's a pro. Have to be careful.

She kept his last known position in her mind and moved quickly towards the other man. The tension was rising in her. She could feel it, the adrenaline rush that preceded the final clash.

But the pressure from the barwolves was building, too.

Emotion: desire to join the pack.

Emotion: negative.

Emotion: strong desire to join. Pleading to join.

Emotion: NO!

She was brought back to re-ti by a rush of soft footsteps behind her, and before she could refocus and turn, an arm slipped around her neck. She grabbed at it, feeling corded muscles, as the arm slid over the collar of her flak vest into the perfect position for a chokehold impossible to break.

She lashed back with her heel and missed. She drove her elbow into a stomach that felt like concrete.

Nzinga...

Emotion: helpless rush. Image: auguar frantically dodging around corners, down alleys.

Her vision was narrowing, darkness closing in on her.

Toni! What's going on? Your signal is fading and Nzinga is frantic

And then all consciousness was washed out by a flood of rage and desire.

Emotion: FEAR AND ANGER! PROTECTION OF THE PACK!

A burst of energy filled her body. Her vision returned. With one hand she plucked the arm from around her neck, hunched her shoulders and threw the man in an overhead toss that landed him, not flat on the ground as she expected, but spread-eagled against the wall at the end of the corridor. He struck with a dull splat, then slid down to lie in a boneless, motionless sprawl at the foot of the wall.

Emotion: triumph and desire to kill!

Andrew, help!

What's going on? The barwolf gestalt has gone wild.

I triggered them, or Nzinga did. Help me shut them down. GET THEM OUT OF MY HEAD!

Through a haze of red she registered Nzinga skidding to a stop, throwing her shoulder against the Pride Leader's leg, her mind burning.

Emotion: REJECTION. OUT! MINE!

Image: Queen Nzinga standing tall. Barwolves slinking away.

Emotion: GO!

In the background Andrew and the *Diablo* gestalt were giving all the support they could. Toni steeled her mind and forced her will on the huge, solidifying mass that surrounded her. Gradually, with far more difficulty than she had peeled the man's arm off her neck, she forced them away, broke their gestalt apart, separated them.

As the weaker pack members succumbed, the power of the gestalt wavered, then disappeared like puff of smoke.

She came to awareness of her surroundings to see a man standing at the end of the corridor, a pistol in his hand, his eyes wavering between the enemy facing him and his partner moaning on the floor.

Toni's sidearm came into line without her conscious thought. "You're the last one left. Battle's over."

The guard only needed one glance at the auguar, now taking her first gliding steps towards him. He pointed his pistol at the ceiling, jacked the chamber open and stooped to lay it on the floor.

"Good choice. See to your partner."

"Aye, ma'am." He crouched to take a pulse.

Away team to Diablo. All secure here.

Glad to hear your voice without all that static, Lieutenant. What went on down there?

Talk about it later in private. Let's secure this facility.

Right you are. Troops in the main airlock now.

Possible medical emergency in the far west end of the storage room. Bring a stretcher.

Alison's the closest thing we have to a medic. Sending her and Achmed in. The Outback pilots will secure the rest of the building and take care of Jackson's captives.

Thanks. I think I'd better look in on the barwolves.

Be careful. That was unnerving.

For you, maybe. For me it was terrifying. Also addictive. Tell you about it later.

Soon she could feel the air pressure change, and hear the tread of feet descending the stairs.

"Over here, Jackson."

"On my way." A pause. "Where the hell are you?"

"Centre of the maze. Follow the right-hand wall until you hit cement. Turn left and follow that to the second-last alley."

"Got it."

The moment he showed up, she flicked her fingers to indicate the two prisoners. He nodded, and she headed for the habitation floor.

As she came down the lab hallway, the augment pressure started to build again, but now she knew how to handle it. She was beginning to recognize individual signatures, and she picked out the weakest ones, pulling them aside and dominating them. Even as she worked, she could feel that it was easier this time. Their gestalt was not so desperate. It was as if they knew the battle was over.

Emotion: calm, peaceful.

Image: tall men in lab coats. Emotion: question?

Image: men in lab coats on floor, tied up

137

Emotion: satisfaction.

Emotion: calm waiting.

Emotion: agreement.

She and Nzinga stood, side by side, just inside the lab door. Her attention on the gestalt was torn away by the acrid smell of uncleaned pens. Shaking it off and breathing in tiny gasps, they assessed the room. Fifty pairs of eyes stared back at them.

Image: two-legged upright being beside Queen Nzinga. Emotion: question?

Image: Pride Leader beside Queen Nzinga

Emotion: disbelief.

Image: Queen Nzinga touching Pride Leader's leg with her paw.

Image: Queen Nzinga's lip lifting in the beginning of a snarl at barwolves.

Emotion: Agreement.

Image: great silver beast with barwolf cubs at his feet. Silver beast playing with cubs, who chew at his feet. Emotion: satisfaction.

At least half the barwolves were now lying in their cages, and the power of their gestalt waned and disappeared again. Toni got the distinct impression that there was one last voice that waited until the rest were gone before it, too, shut down. She glanced along the curved line of cages, but none of the creatures were looking at her.

"Well, done, Nzinga. Let's go tidy up." She closed the lab door and took deep, gasping breaths of the clean air of the hallway. "First order of business is venting that lab."

15.   UP AND OUT

They sat around *Diablo's* cramped mess, looking at each other in satisfaction. Andrew leaned his arms on the table. "Well, what do we do, now?"

Toni took a moment. "We've got one Martin on patrol, one pilot on the monitors in Security Control, and one off duty. We can rotate that until our backup arrives in two days. The SolarCorp staff are fine in their rooms. They're too scared of their former victims to want to escape."

"Which brings us to our clients. We have a troop transport coming to repatriate them. It's a multi-cabin job, so we can keep them in small groups. All we have to do is get in there and bring them out one at a time."

Morissa shook her head. "I'm sorry, Andrew, but we have a much larger problem than that."

He stared at her. "We do? In what way?"

"Up and out, remember?" She gave him a small smile. "I'm looking long-term."

He leaned back in his chair. "The floor is yours, ma'am. What's the deal?"

"We cannot just dump these individuals back into the general population. First, we don't know where they came from, and I doubt if they do either. It would be interesting to try, of course, because it would indicate their level of sophistication, if they were aware of the geography of the planet.

"But that's not the biggest problem. In terms of my study, these subjects have been contaminated. Given the conditions they were placed in, they may not even be sane."

Toni nodded. "They were under a great deal of stress. Nzinga and I could hardly bear it ourselves. They were being forced into a situation that normally would have induced a panic reaction but not allowed their normal outlet for that rage. They were held in that situation for...what, weeks? Months, some of them? We have no idea what they will do if we turn them free. That huge, vague pack mind has had the experience, if only for a moment, of focus. What if it manages that again on its own?"

"We've already had this conversation." Andrew shook his head. "There is no guarantee they haven't been stimulated into a new stage of their evolution."

Alison Rowell had been sitting back, listening, but now she leaned forward. "I don't understand a lot of this, but what I'm hearing is frightening. It sounds like we have a potentially insane hive mind that could, if allowed to spread, encompass this whole species and turn it into a single ravaging entity with no reason to love the Human race."

Andrew regarded her. "You have such a pleasant way of stating the problem. Do you have a solution?"

She shook her head. "You all know the easy one, but no one here has the guts to say it, let alone do the deed."

Morissa's face clouded. "What do you mean, an easy solution?"

Toni sighed. "The military solution to a situation that dangerous to the human race is to make it like it never existed. We pull out of here and slam a Sidewinder missile through the airlock as we go." She dusted her hands. "End of threat, end of scientists, end of illegal research. We go back to studying our pristine subjects."

The scientist was on her feet. "No! You can't even think of that. It's too...too..." she waved her hands in frustration. Then she spun and pointed at Toni. "It's too dangerous. I need the knowledge base those scientists have developed. I need these barwolves, because they're our only chance to discover what contact with Humanity might do to them. You can't just destroy them!"

There was a moment of silence, then the sound of solo applause. Andrew stopped clapping and nodded at the stricken woman. "Job well done. Looking out and ahead." He hitched his chair forward. "We have to be aware of the danger we're facing, and take appropriate steps.

"The way I see this, we could go down two dangerous paths. First, we react too quickly and, as Morissa points out, destroy valuable research possibilities. And incidentally get us into a whole passel of trouble for murdering both humans and possibly other intelligent beings. The second mistake is if we let this virus go and it causes the end of Humanity as we know it. We'll go down in history as the plague bearers. Of course, I doubt we'll be around to experience the fallout, but I'd still rather not."

"So," he spread his hand to include the whole group, "any ideas? No pressure, but just one genius plan to save two races from extinction might be nice."

There was silence in the tiny room.

He smiled. "That's fine. Let's not rush into this."

Another silence, broken by a plaintive "Myerouw" from Nzinga.

Image: barwolves in cages. Emotion: great sorrow.

"Yes, love. I'll tell them." Toni gazed around the room. "If there's any way we can reduce the pain those creatures are going through..."

Andrew shrugged. "The only solution that might work is reducing their numbers. Everything we know about augment communication is that it drops off with the square of the distance, and we are assuming that gestalt power drops off something like exponentially as number of members decreases. If we could move any of them any distance at all...well, every little bit counts."

Morissa was thinking. "Toni, is there any quick way of telling the mental state of an individual?"

"Perhaps. When we met that pack back on the Tree Planet, I barely got anything from them. Now, their gestalt shouts at me, and I'm learning to pick out single voices in it, so maybe I can talk to individuals. We'd have to remove them from that room, though."

Andrew jumped to his feet. "That's a big enough facility to have space. Let's clean out a couple of bedrooms at opposite ends of that hallway and leave them with water and mattresses. That will only give them twenty or thirty metres of separation, but any little bit helps. Who knows, maybe the stimulus is visual? You can figure out a way to sort them, and we'll get a few of them spread around."

"Easy for you to say." She stopped beside him. "You won't be down there sorting."

"Was it that bad?" He put a hand on her shoulder, leaning down to look into her eyes.

"Andrew, you know better than anyone what it's like when you're in the gestalt. Information at your fingertips. Vision in the micro and the macro. You feel like a super-human."

He nodded. "Which you are."

"Well, this was ten times that. I tell you, I could have counted the atoms in the sleeve of that guy's shirt as I pulled it off my neck. He weighs a hundred and twenty kilos at least, and I tossed him end over end. He hit the wall a meter up. Lucky for him it was plastic. If he'd hit cement he'd have a concussion if not a broken neck."

"Want me to come along?"

"Definitely not." She reached up and ran a finger down his nose. "You just stay in your little ship where you're safe and warm."

She gave a sharp push to the tip of his nose, then snatched her finger back before he could grab it, stood and headed for the doorway out of the lounge.

Once the rooms were prepared, the others returned to the ship, and the pilots stayed on patrol in the hallways.

When everything was secure, she and Nzinga cautiously entered the lab. The barwolves were all on their feet, silent, staring at them. It took her a moment to focus, as her eyes were watering from the acrid atmosphere. Exhaust fans hummed, but the smell was still overpowering.

Emotion: curiosity, wariness. Emotion: vast, seething anger and frustration.

Toni twined her fingers in Nzinga's neck fur.

Emotion: calm, sympathy.

Emotion: hesitant, suspicious acceptance.

The two stepped forward, heading for the right-hand end of the arc of cages.

As they moved, Toni felt Nzinga's picture of the gestalt. Where before it had been an amorphous mass, now it was clearer, and she could distinguish individual swirls of difference. The first creature they approached spiked in barely contained fear, and they stepped back quickly and moved on. The next two did not stand out among the others, but the fourth one was different. This was a taller specimen, but slim. The armour was smoother and not so scarred as the others.

A young one?

Emotion: agreement.

Toni reached out a hand and a greeting.

Emotion: curiosity, cautious acceptance.

Gradually, she moved her hand until it rested on the latch of the door.

Emotion: invitation.

Emotion: eager acceptance.

Emotion: concern.

Emotion: reassurance.

Image: huge queen auguar in ferocious stance. Strong emotion: dominance!

Emotion: Subservience. Image: hoofed paw touching foreleg of auguar.

Emotion: satisfaction.

Slowly, Toni unlocked the cage, opened the door and stepped back.

Just as slowly, the young auguar slid forward, its blunt head questing. It stepped out, first one forepaw, then the other, the hard hoof making a light clicking sound on the floor plates.

When the creature was fully out of the cage, it knelt and touched Toni's leg. She began to move slowly towards the door.

Invitation: freedom.

The barwolf hesitated. *Emotion: negative.*

143

Emotion: gentle command.

Emotion: desperate negative.

Emotion: firm command!

Easy, Nzinga. There's something we don't understand, here. Something's wrong, and she can't tell us. What is she afraid of?

Emotion: question?

The barwolf slid forward, its belly to the floor, and touched Nzinga's leg with her paw. Then it rose and moved backward, toward the other cages.

She wants us to do something.

Image: all cage doors open.

Emotion: great fear.

Emotion: agreement.

Image: one cage door open.

Emotion: agreement.

Image: two cage doors open.

Toni widened her augment. *Andrew, are you getting this? We're having a real conversation.*

Morissa reminds you that this is possibly a trigender species.

She returned her attention to the barwolf.

Image: two doors open.

Emotion: cautious acceptance. Emotion: question?

Now the barwolf moved with more assurance. She stopped in front of another cage, where a smaller member of the species stood eagerly at the door, dancing like a puppy at feeding time. The larger one touched noses through the bars, then stood aside, looking at Toni.

Emotion: pleading.

Okay, kid. Stand back, please, both of you. Here goes.

The barwolves understood, and both moved away from the front of the cage.

Toni undid the latch, opened the door and jumped out of the way.

The smaller creature barrelled out, leaping straight to its friend, slamming shoulder to shoulder, almost knocking both of them to the floor. It bounced off and pushed against the other, rubbing their armour-coated shoulders together with a grating sound.

Emotions: calm, danger, worry.

The smaller barwolf would have none of it. With one more playful surge against its partner's shoulder, it bounced to a cage at the other end of the row, coming up with a loud clang against the door. Then it turned and bounded halfway back to Toni, crouching on its belly.

Emotion: pleasepleaseplease?

Toni laughed. *Young love at its barwolf finest?*

Andrew chuckled. Or puppy stupidity. Morissa says this is the first sign of normal behaviour she's seen in this group.

Well, going on the mathematics, once we get three of them out here the odds go way up of something even crazier happening. Here goes.

She walked across and looked into the third cage. The barwolf inside was shorter as well, but this one was stockier. It had heavy armour, more scratched and knotted than either of the other two.

Well, buddy, I hope you're the sober elder statesman of the group.

She undid the clasp and stood back.

This barwolf reacted with more dignity. It strode out the door and approached Toni directly. Lowering itself to the floor, it touched her leg. Then it repeated the action with Nzinga.

Emotion: great gratitude.

Only then did it rise and greet its family. The second barwolf had remained low, quivering with anxiety and the suppressed need to move. As its partner approached, it jumped up and stood, head down.

Emotion: suppressed anxiety, fear, love.

The older barwolf walked past and at the last moment twitched its hindquarters, sending the lighter creature off balance. It reacted immediately, scrabbling to its feet and running along the face of the other cages in a great circle, spewing happiness, relief, love, and a whole lot of emotional gibberish.

The two other members greeted each other with more dignity, noses overlapping each other's withers for all the world like horses in the shade on a hot day. Then they turned and approached Toni and stood in front of her, shoulder to shoulder, looking up.

Emotion: question?

Image: small, quiet room with open door. Emotion: question?

Emotion: agreement

Toni and Nzinga led the way down the residence hall to the corner bedroom. The taller of the barwolves entered first and circled the room.

Emotion: satisfaction.

The other two entered and also gazed around.

Emotion: dissatisfaction.

The two shorter creatures walked over to the matresses and, taking one end each, picked the first up and set it neatly on top of the other. Then all three jumped on; in a melee of legs and loudly scraping bodies, they settled themselves into one pile of barwolf flesh.

Emotion: satisfaction.

Question: quiet?

Emotion: negative. Emotion: gratitude.

I think that means it's not much better, but thanks for trying.

Toni, will you go back to the lab and monitor the others?

Roger that.

The two walked back down the hallway. Now that she was getting used to it, Toni could feel the increase in mental pressure as she approached the combined pack, but it didn't bother her as much.

She stopped just inside the doorway, appalled again by the smell. It was worse than any barn she had ever been in. She focused on her job. Now the creatures were less focused, standing or lying in various positions in their cages, but all looking at her.

Emotion: question?

There was no response, only a feeling of confusion. Toni thought a moment.

Image: three barwolves exiting cages, moving to the door. Emotion: question?

No clear response.

Image: two barwolves leaving cages. Emotion: question?

This time there were responses, too mixed to understand. None seemed to have the drive of the first family. She tried again.

Image: two barwolves leaving cages. Emotion: question?

This time the answer was clear, and led them to another tall barwolf. This one looked older than the rest, with a slight droop to its backbone and heavy, scarred armour. It immediately stood back from the door, and she let it out. It glanced at her, briefly touched Nzinga's leg, then moved with a slight limp to a cage where another old barwolf lay.

When the door was open, this creature looked up but did not move.

Emotion: great sorrow.

The first barwolf entered the cage and lay beside its mate. There was no question that tragedy had struck this duo. Wondering whether her emotions were going to make her do something she would regret later, she left the door open and went to the next prisoners that attracted her.

This pair seemed to be in the middle age range and they followed the routine with obedience, if no enthusiasm.

Just as Toni was about to close the lab door, there was a disturbance in the larger gestalt. One voice seemed determined to attract her attention. She turned back.

Emotion: question?

Emotion: determined plea.

She glanced into the room. Now the focus of the pack's attention was on a cage in the corner, separate from the rest. The barwolf inside was black, brown and yellow in a brindle pattern, and smaller than most of the others. It was standing, face pressed against the bars, eyes burning with desire, even fervour.

"Okay, pal, I'll be back." *Image: human and auguar returning.*

Emotion: satisfaction.

With the other pair settled in the last room, she returned to the lab. The solo barwolf was pacing its cage, rasping its armour against the bars. When she and Nzinga entered, it stopped and stared at them again, pushing its emotional plea with every ounce of its physical body.

Andrew, I've got a live one down here.

Morissa says it's worth looking into. Be careful, though.

Toni strode to the cage, looking down at its occupant.

Emotion: question.

Emotion: frantic plea. Image: door opening, barwolf leaving, barwolf, belly to floor, touching Nzinga's leg.

What do you think, Nzinga? It seems very anxious.

The auguar strolled over and stuck her nose through the bars. The barwolf crouched to the floor, staring up with none of the cringing attitude the others had displayed.

Nzinga batted the lock with one paw, and the latch sprang open.

The barwolf shouldered through the door and then, as promised, paid homage to first Nzinga, then Toni.

Fine. But what are we going to do with you? We don't have another room.

Image. Toni walking out, Nzinga on one side, barwolf on the other.

Andrew, this one wants to hire on. Its communication is very clear. What does Morissa suggest?

She says it would be in keeping with her revered ancestor's methods. But don't give it a name until we can figure out what the reproductive pattern is. We don't want a boy named Sue wandering around camp.

Okay, I had to look that one up. Ha, ha. So, am I bringing it onboard?

I think you have to. If you leave it loose in the lab it's likely to turn the rest free.

Roger. I think I've done all I can down here. We've removed six from the group, so that reduces the pressure somewhat. The main effect is that the gestalt has definitely settled. There hasn't been a riot since we took over, you notice.

Fair enough. Bring your new friend onboard, and we'll start with the toilet training.

Don't worry, Nzinga's a bit of a clean freak. She'll get the message across.

Fine. Jackson will take command of the facility. Come on up.

On my way.

16. ALIEN HUSBANDRY

The following morning, they held a meeting in the lounge of the lab. The full SolarCorp staff was there, and all the Space Arm personnel who weren't on guard duty. Andrew was about to start, but stopped because no one was looking at him. They were all observing three heavy snouts sticking in the door.

Andrew spoke aloud for the benefit of the others.

"Sure, this is a meeting for everyone. Go sit with Brindle and Nzinga over there, and she can translate."

To everyone's amusement and surprise, that's exactly what they did, forming their usual pile of intertwined limbs. The auguar lay down beside them, not quite touching. Her new friend had already found a spot nearby, from which it stared at everyone through bright brown eyes.

"All right, everyone. Here's the situation. Our backup is on its way, but it won't be here for a while. We're not outfitted to keep our pilots in their craft, you SolarCorp folks have to live your lives and the barwolves have to be taken care of."

He regarded the scientists and guards. "There's two ways to do this. First we keep you all in your rooms, locked up tight the full time. We let the chef out under supervision to cook your meals. We do all the work, and since we don't really know how to take care of barwolves, we might make some mistakes. It will be a very unpleasant few days.

"The other choice is that we all pitch in together and keep this place running as normally as possible. You'll be taking care of your guests, but it won't be as usual. Because of the possibility that they are an intelligent species," he stared at the scientists until their eyes dropped, "and because we are reasonable caring human beings, there will be some changes made. What's your choice?"

He looked at an older man, hefty and red-faced. "You look like you have something to say. Who are you?"

150

The scientist heaved himself to his feet, making it look difficult despite the lack of serious gravity. "I'm Dr. Johannes Flagstaff, and I'm in charge of this base. What about our research?"

"I don't know. Tell me about your illegal research on a protected species kidnapped from a prohibited planet?"

While the doctor was protesting about his complete lack of knowledge of the illegality of anything and bemoaning the loss of proper scientific isolation for his very difficult subjects, Toni accessed *Diablo's* data banks. She used Nzinga's talents to bring the information up on a tablet, which she placed in front of Morissa with the words, 'What do you think?' on it.

The answer came quickly. "If he is who he says he is, he knows what he's talking about."

Without comment, Toni slipped the message into Andrew's augment.

By this time the scientist had run out of complaints, so Andrew regarded him. "Well, Dr. Flagstaff, it is possible that your data might have use to the Space Arm investigation into this species and their potential classification of intelligent."

"Intelligent? Nonsense. Perhaps a bit more intuitive than the common timber wolf, but nowhere near up there with the Orcas. And so violent, even towards each other, I'm not certain how the species hasn't destroyed itself long ago."

"Well, this is Dr. Morissa Goodall of the South African College of Applied Psychology, and her research has progressed much further than yours. However, considering the charges against you, if you want to redeem yourself in any small way, I suggest you cooperate with her with all your cold little heart. Do I take it that you are all in agreement, then?"

"I refuse to be treated like a criminal!"

"Then don't act like one, and all will be well." He glanced at the three security guards. "Any problem with that, fellas?"

The crew chief shook his bandaged head. "We were hired to do a job. We had no idea what it was all about. Sort of glad it's over, come to think of it."

"Fine. Looks like your job just got classified up one level." He grinned at the cook. "Any of these three look like a possible flunky?"

The black-skinned man shrugged. "They're all ex-military. They've peeled a spud or two, I imagine."

"Good. And once again, I'm taking your parole you won't try to poison us. We'll all be eating the same food, and so far, you're the only one here that isn't facing charges."

"Oh, don't worry about me, sir. I do my job proper no matter what. Point of pride."

"Well, since this base is probably about to be shut down in the next month or so, knock yourself out. Anything you were saving for a special occasion, let's have it, or it's probably meant for the permanent deep-freeze out there. Why don't you dismiss yourself from this meeting and think about lunch at, say, 12 hundred hours?"

"I could probably manage something." He started away, then turned back. "Any way I can keep various uninvited intelligent creatures out of my kitchen?"

"If you don't want them there, ask them to leave."

"You're serious?"

"If you're talking about the barwolves, they understand more of what humans are saying than you might think. If you mean the Space Arm pilots, I'm not so sure. Let me know if anyone gets in your way. A happy cook makes a happy ship."

The cook looked rather flustered, and turned and headed for his galley with a lift to his step.

Andrew regarded the rest of the group. "Now that the important stuff is out of the way, we have our clients to think of. Who was looking after them?"

Blank looks passed between the scientists.

"The barwolves! Who fed them, watered them, mucked out their cages?"

The light dawned, and two younger men held up their hands. On, a tall, scrawny sort with a long neck and equally straggly hair stood. "I'm Joachim Perez. Bill and I took care of them, sir. Dr. Flagstaff set the routine, and we followed it exactly. It was all completely regulated, you know, all scientifically controlled."

The other, a shorter, heavier boy, stuck up a hesitant hand. "William Anderson, sir. But we didn't actually muck out the cages. Wouldn't dare."

"Which is why the lab stinks so badly." Andrew's eyes turned towards Flagstaff. "Tell me, if you were keeping such careful scientific controls in place, how do you think the mess in there mimics their natural environment?"

The scientist's shoulders squared. "You do the best you can. It wasn't our choice. A variable we couldn't control, and a product of the vicious nature of the beast."

Andrew glanced pointedly at the heap of snoozing barwolves. "Yes, yes I can see it would be a problem."

"But..."

"It's all right, Doctor. I know all about your problems, and I know how to solve them."

"You...you do?"

"Toni, will you send your new friend over here?"

Image: barwolf goes to Pride Leader

The brindled creature got up, stretched and strolled over to lie at Andrew's side, tapping his leg with a casual forepaw as he did.

"This barwolf has been on my ship for twelve hours. During that time, it has learned to operate the head, the feeding station and, unfortunately for us, the music sound system, which it enjoys immensely at high volume. I gather a sense of hearing is not a strength in this species. It came back here early this morning, and if you note the rooms our guests are staying in, it has also taught them the benefits of a low-grav toilet."

He indicated the two junior scientists. "Bill and Joachim will go with Lieutenant Jacobs, who will see to their security and the adaptation of their routines to a more satisfactory sanitary level."

Gee, thanks, boss.

153

Two young and handsome assistants? I thought you'd thank me.

I just did.

She rose and gestured them to follow. As they walked down the hall, she introduced them to Nzinga. "You know what an auguar is."

"Of course! Everybody in the social sciences wants to know about them. A real bonus, running into one way out here."

"Try to make it stay that way. What's your training?"

"I'm working on my Master's in Xenosociology." His face fell. "At least I was. Shortage of funds. Had to take a job, and this one looked very promising."

"Hmm. Until you got here and discovered it was cleaning out barwolf cages. Which you didn't." She pulled open the door and the smell washed over them. As they entered, the feeling of the gestalt changed. Every barwolf was on its feet, now, and there were plenty of teeth inevidence.

Nzinga...

Emotion: calmness, safety.

The emotional level dropped, and the teeth disappeared.

"How did you do that?"

"First lesson in auguars, Joachim. She communicates with them through her augment."

"You don't say. I've got an augment. Top-of-the line eight point three. Well... not top of the line. But the best I could afford."

"Your bad luck. Only organics work."

"Only organics? Well, what do you know?"

The brindle barwolf pushed ahead, making the circuit of the cages. It seemed to be communing with each creature. As it passed they calmed even further. But it stopped at the cage containing the older pair and stood there, gazing in.

"Oh, that one. Yeah, I figure it's not long for this world. Why'd you put the other one in there? Hey, the door's open!"

"Because it requested that they be together."

"What? What do you mean, requested?"

"Well, the bigger one walked to the cage, and when I opened the door, it walked in. Non-verbal communication isn't rocket science, you know."

"I never had the chance. I was too busy trying not to rile them up."

"And so you never did your job properly. Look at the mess on the floor."

The cages were raised a few centimetres, with half their floor made of mesh, on the assumption that waste materials would drop through and be hosed away. From the look of it, barwolf feces were rather fluid, so that part had worked. They were also as odiferous as most carnivorous waste is.

"All right. Where's the cleaning stuff? Let's get at this."

They showed her the rubber boots and gloves and then hooked up the hoses. As the water was turned on, the barwolves rose in their cages, pacing.

Bill, who had just started to work, turned his hose away. "Watch out. They're starting."

Toni checked the gestalt. The feeling was rising, but altogether different from before. "No, they aren't. Look at them."

"They're pacing. That's what they do before they go ape."

"It's not the same. Give me a hose." She stepped forward and pointed the stream of water at the floor.

"Watch out, Lieutenant!"

A brindle body dove in front of her, grabbing at the water with pointed teeth. She jerked the hose away, but the barwolf followed, biting at the water stream again.

She played the hose in a different direction, and once more the creature followed, this time running its shoulder through it.

She shut the hose off and looked at the two dumbfounded scientists. "It's playing with the water! Haven't you ever seen a dog with a hose on a hot day?"

"Huh? Oh, sure, I guess."

"So now, let's put those sharp scientific minds to their proper use. Why are the barwolves pacing back and forth?"

"Because they like it? They want to be sprayed?"

"What else? Say, let's try something. *Nzinga, tell it to come over here.*

Obediently the brindle barwolf stood in front of her, its mouth gaping in invitation. She turned on the hose at a lower rate and played it on the creature's chest and shoulders. It turned sideways.

Question: cold?

Emotion: cold.

"Bill, give me a bit of warm in this. Not too much."

Question: cold?

Emotion: cold.

"A bit more."

Question: cold?

Emotion: warm! Joy!

The barwolf positively wriggled, turning its body so that all parts were washed.

She handed the hose to Joachim. "There you go. Set both hoses at that temperature. Wash the floor, wash the cages, and wash the barwolves. I'm sure you can figure out how much pressure they like. They've got heavy skin, so they might take a lot. Maybe they're upset because they're itchy." She regarded their astonished faces. "They're aliens. Keep an open mind."

Once the hose was turned away from it, the brindle barwolf tossed the drops of water off by jumping up and coming down stiff-legged. Then it strolled over to the door and lay down to watch the show. Even the dying barwolf staggered to its feet and turned once to get completely cleaned off. When it lay down again, Bill turned wondering eyes to Toni, then returned to his work.

Toni didn't see any need to supervise this, so she took off her boots and gloves and went to the door. *Keep an ear open for trouble in their gestalt, Nzinga. Come along, both of you.*

She opened the door, and they followed her out.

In the hallway, two astonished scientists were staring through the one-way observation glass.

"Seems they like water."

"Yes, it does. But how did you find out?"

She regarded them for a moment. "Doctor, I'm a Commando. We communicate by hand signals all the time, so I'm used to non-verbal communication, I guess. But I don't think that's the problem. Are you familiar with Dr. Goodall's work?"

"Oh, yes. She's very respected in the field. But some, at any rate."

"But not by others. That figures. Well, I learned something from her that she learned from her ancestor. If you look at something and assume you understand it, you will only see evidence confirming what you think you know." She tossed a thumb over her shoulder at the window. "Those boys got out the hoses, and the barwolves became active. They assumed the barwolves were getting upset. They shut off the hoses because the barwolves were rioting. So the barwolves rioted because the water was being taken away. So, they proved themselves correct by perfectly acceptable scientific experimentation. Which was completely wrong."

Flagstaff's face began to redden. "And you're telling me that my work has been similarly skewed?"

She raised her eyebrows. "I'm a soldier. I've never seen your research. How can I tell you anything?"

She started to turn away, but he raised a hand to stop her. "That barwolf. The brindle one."

She looked down. "Oh, this one. Yes, it's different. No doubt about it. You already had its cage off by itself."

"That's right. We couldn't put it near any of the others. They went nuts. Even more than usual. Why is it loose?"

"Because it asked to be. No, don't look at me like that. My auguar communicates with it, but I didn't need help to know that this creature had a greater desire to be free than the others. And when it's free, it walks in there and calms the others down."

"It does? No. That can't be. It's completely the opposite."

157

She consulted her augment. "I assume you keep a re-ti record of this lab. Check the images from twenty-seven minutes ago, when we first entered the room."

The doctor regarded her. "Thank you, Lieutenant Jacobs. I appreciate your point of view. If I'm allowed to continue with this research, can I count on you and your auguar to…" he created a weak smile… "keep me from going off track?"

She answered with a smile of her own. "I have absolutely no influence over that decision, but if you're working with Dr. Goodall's project, my resources are available. My auguar, of course, is a classified Space Arm project, so information on her would be limited."

"Of course, of course. Thank you, Lieutenant."

"You're welcome, Doctor."

She turned down the hall, leaving him to bustle about with his recording equipment.

17.   RESCUE

Two days later a troop carrier from the embassy showed up with ten Space Arm Marines aboard. Their leader was Major Sergei Bykov, newly arrived from Earth, an imposing man in a medal-bedecked, razor-creased uniform.

Nzinga sat at Toni's feet, regarding him with slitted eyes.

Apparently it was a good thing he finally showed up, because in his opinion this operation, run by female junior officers and civilians, was going rapidly downhill. He had obviously never heard Captain O'Rourke's lecture on the value of experience in the Outback. The first problem was the creatures running loose all over the base.

"I really must protest, Mr. Collingwood. It is impossible to expect my men to conduct proper security exercises when there are doors that must remain open, doors that must remain closed, and these... animals running all over the place."

"Yes, it's a good thing you got here, Major Bykov, because now we can divide up the pack into a size that won't cause any trouble."

"What are you talking about?"

Andrew put on the look of surprise that Toni knew meant trouble for his opponent. "Haven't you read your briefing notes?"

"Of course. I'm to come out here, provide security for the operation until it is over, then transport twenty of these barwolves back to the Tree Planet."

Andrew nodded. "And these orders were written by whom?"

"By my commanding officer, of course. Why is that any business of yours?"

"Because the person who wrote the orders probably doesn't have the security clearance to know what's really going on here. In fact, I'm not sure you have the level necessary to even set foot in this base. Not much of a problem, though. You just have some of the timelines a little skewed."

The broad brow furrowed. "Skewed?"

"Yes. The reason we needed a multi-cabin long-range troop carrier is that we don't have any other resource available in the system to house a group of our clients. It is essential for their welfare that we house them away from the base as quickly as possible."

"I...suppose that is possible. Who are these clients?"

"The barwolves."

"What?"

"That's right. Lieutenant Jacobs is our expert at liaison with our clients."

He nodded to Toni, who returned the nod and motioned the Major to follow her. She led the way down the hall and opened the lab door.

Bykov's face screwed up. "This is a foul place."

"You should have seen it before we cleaned it up." She grinned. "Who would have known the barwolves like to be hosed off?"

"No, not the room. These animals. They reek of evil."

"Evil?"

"Can't you feel it? No, you probably can't. These animals are the embodiment of evil." He glanced down at her. "No...no, I'm sorry. I know how that sounded. I don't mean evil in a religious sense. I mean malevolent. They are alien and have no reason for good will towards Humanity. Can't you feel it?"

Toni shook her head. "It's becoming an open secret, and I think you need some information if you're to do your job. These creatures communicate through something like an organic augment. The messages they are sending are perceptible to any Space Arm officer with above a Standard eight-point-five-level augment. You are correct in saying they have no reason for good will." She gestured around the room. "They have been kidnapped from their native homes and brought to this."

"I see...."

"The other factor is that forcing them together in large numbers triggers a killing frenzy, and they destroy each other. They have been kept in close proximity for five weeks or more.

We are not sure whether all of them are completely sane. So, if you're getting a sense of hatred from them, you're probably right, and we deserve it.

"It's our duty and to our self-interest to alleviate their condition as quickly as possible, and the first step in that is to remove at least twenty of them from the immediate vicinity. Your troop carrier is the solution. That's why you were sent in a vessel of that configuration. I assume two large cabins, at opposite ends of the ship, are completely stripped of furniture?"

"They are."

"Padded floors and walls?

"Yes..."

"Now you know why."

"I see. Well, that does put things in a different light."

"I'm glad you see it that way. Can we start preparing for the transfer?"

"Not right away. I thank you for your input, Lieutenant...Jacobs, isn't it? Yes. I will take it into consideration when I make my decision."

Nzinga, I caught that! You will not urinate on this man's shoes.

Emotion: reluctant agreement.

She turned to the door. "Well, you've seen everything you need to see here, sir. Perhaps you understand why we have barwolves housed in different parts of the complex. Anything to keep them as spread out as possible. You should talk to Dr. Goodall. She can fill you in from a scientific point of view."

"Yes, yes I suppose I should." He preceded her out and she followed, resisting the urge to drive her fist into his right kidney at the precise angle to cause internal bleeding and eventual death. To distract herself, she contacted Andrew. *Thanks for dumping me with this guy.*

I figured your mature demeanour would carry more weight.

It didn't. What are we going to do?

No idea. I'd hate to have to call for help.

Me, too. Well, over to Morissa.

Let me know. Worse comes to worst, turn him over to Nzinga. She'll straighten him around.

Tempting thought. She already tried to urinate on his shoes.

Not a technique I would have thought of, but I'll file it in my bag of tricks.

We might get that desperate. Not looking forward to this meeting.

However, she had not counted on Morissa's dedication to her task.

When they reached the lab office, the scientist looked up. "Hi, Toni. When can we start the transfers?"

Toni said nothing, nodding to Major Bykov, who frowned.

"I'm not sure that would serve the best interests of the expedition, ma'am."

Her brow darkened. "Pardon me?"

Unaware, he forged on. "Well, it seems to me that this operation has been running on a very ad hoc basis, with no ranking officer to keep it all on track. I think we should sit down and have a meeting..."

Her voice softened, her eyes wide. "Major, excuse me a moment. Why would this expedition need a ranking military officer?"

Toni grinned to herself. *She's been taking lessons from Andrew.*

"Well, to organize it, of course."

"Oh. And you consider this a military expedition, do you?"

He frowned in surprise. "Of course."

Now the steel was beginning to show in Morissa's spine. "Well, if you look around you, I think you will find exactly five Space Arm crew in this expedition." She counted them off on her fingers. "Two of them, with their ships, have been seconded to my operation by Admiral Mira. Two of them with special skills for liason with my clients have been assigned to me by Ambassador Pretoro. One, in case nobody thought to warn you, is the ambassador's special envoy, here to give me any assistance he can."

162

She stared at him a moment. "And if counting was included in your obviously faulty military training, you will see that leaves exactly zero military people in the expedition for you to organize except your men." She stood. "And if you do not come up to scratch in the accomplishment of that duty, I'm sure Lieutenant Jacobs is more than capable of filling in until you are replaced."

A frown crossed her brow. "Of course, we have no way to send you back, so I suppose we'd just throw you in with the prisoners to keep you from causing any disturbance. Or maybe the barwolves. But I doubt they would appreciate that."

She sat down and spun her office chair back to face her desk, speaking over her shoulder. "Toni, please arrange directly with the IPC pilot to match his airlock with the station's, STAT. And would you go aboard personally and see that the cabins are arranged properly for their passengers?"

She looked up at Bykov from her relaxed pose as if surprised he was still there. "That will be all, Major. I'll let you know the duties required of your men, and you can make up a schedule."

Toni tipped two fingers to her brow at Morissa and spun out the door, leaving the man standing, his mouth agape.

Once the IPC was connected, Toni brought Joachim and Bill to help her set up the rooms. They took the doors off the toilet cubicles, moved feeding troughs from the lab and bolted them in, and arranged the heavy foam matting that covered the floor. Bill also attached cannisters of sleeping gas into the individual ventilation systems.

"Thanks, boys. That ought to nail it. Go clear the halls, and I'll start the herding."

Down in the containment lab, she pondered communication.

Image: barwolves divided into groups of ten. Emotion: question?

The brindle barwolf stood in front of her, eyes probing.

Image: ten barwolves. Emotion: Question?

Image: pack of barwolves in Personel Carrier.

Emotion: anger!

163

Image: Pack of barwolves exiting Personel Carrier onto Tree Planet.

Emotion: hesitant question?

Emotion: Affirmation

Emotion: Regal affirmation! Nzinga slunk to a hunting crawl and approached the brindle creature, her neck hairs raised.

It sank to an even lower level and touched her leg.

Immediately she stood tall and strolled around to rub her neck against its armoured shoulder.

Emotion: acceptance.

The barwolf paced down the line of cages. As it passed, some creatures remained standing, others lay down. When it finished, five barwolves waited to be released.

Image: ten barwolves. Emotion: question?

Image: trio of barwolves alone. Image, two barwolves alone.

"Oh, yes." *Emotion: agreement.*

Andrew, I have ten clients ready for transfer and a barwolf that can do simple arithmetic. The ITC is at the airlock. Could you check the route is clear?

Already done.

Great. Nzinga will bring the first one, the Brindle will bring the second, and then we'll see.

I'll be standing by. Proceed.

She opened the cage to let the first standing creature out. It touched her leg and then hesitated, looking towards another barwolf.

Image: two barwolves walking together in forest.

Emotion: agreement.

With a final glance at its partner, the first traveller followed Nzinga out of the door. This had gone so well that she brought out the partner immediately. It followed its brindle compatriot, and Toni trailed with a third, randomly selected from those left standing.

The little procession made it out the airlock and through the troop carrier without incident. As soon as the three were happily curled on the padded decking, she went back to the bedroom and brought out the trio, which curled happily in another corner of the cabin.

Everything going well?

Too smoothly for words.

Then let's not talk; let's get moving.

Aye, Captain Bligh.

As they came back to the lab again, she monitored the barwolf gestalt, which was dropping in power and relaxing. Taking this as a good sign, she thought of opening all four remaining cages and bringing the last group in a pack. Then she reconsidered. *What if there's a problem in the carrier?*

She sent the next two with Nzinga and Brindle, instructing her auguar to stay at the far end. Then she and the lead barwolf brought the last pair from their cabin.

When she reached the new transport room, she hit her augment. *Andrew, I think Morissa will want to see this.*

She's already watching. Think she'd miss an opportunity?

Good.

The barwolves had arranged themselves in four separate groups. The trio and one pair had claimed corners of the room, and the others gave them space. The rest milled about in the centre, a few nibbling at the food that had been left out. But a group of three had claimed a rather large section near the door. Their movements were slow but seemed patterned in some way.

I don't think I should be interfering.

Morissa thanks you for that thought.

Toni looked at the brindle barwolf.

Image: barwolf using low-grav toilet.

Emotion: reassurance.

Emotion: grateful thanks.

She and Nzinga left, latching the door behind them. She would go back and collect her apostle once the group had settled into predictable patterns.

After two hours they repeated the process with the second cabin, and finally they had twenty barwolves installed in their new temporary homes, and thirty more in a very calm state in the lab.

A great loosening of tension permeated the supper hour that night. Even the scientists responsible for the problem were relieved.

In fact, Dr. Flagstaff engaged Morissa in such a long and impassioned conversation that finally Toni strolled close enough to catch the other woman's eye.

At that, Morissa rose. "I'm sorry, Dr. Flagstaff, but it's out of my hands. I cannot see that you would be allowed to take any benefit from the clandestine research you have been doing here. If the barwolves are deemed of lower intelligence, then legitimate scientists from accredited institutions will continue the studies. If they are declared an intelligent species, then it will be social anthropologists dealing with them, and out of your realm of expertise in any case. I will accept any help you can give me in interpreting your data, and I will use my influence with Ambassador Pretoro to take that cooperation into account when he is deciding your fate. But your data will be confiscated by Space Arm, and you will not be allowed intellectual rights over it."

She turned and walked towards Toni, leaving a dejected scientist slouched on the sofa where they had been sitting.

"I guess I know what that was about."

"Yes. I think he overrates the quality of his data and underestimates the moral code of the Planetary Community."

"Fair enough. I wish our other problems were so easily solved."

"So do I."

"Didn't want to spoil your fun, but Andrew wants to meet."

"Now?"

"Yes."

"Let's go."

Diablo had replaced the IPC over the airlock, and they met on the bridge. To Toni's questioning look, Andrew gestured to the large viewscreens. "Conference with Mum and Alfino in ten minutes. Want to grab a tea first?"

18.   RETURN HOME

Soon they were all gathered in *Diablo's* cockpit. Andrew scanned his supporters. "What do we need to ask them about? Jackson, you're looking worried."

"Have you locked down the computer systems?"

Andrew glanced at Toni. "The security levels, yes."

Jackson frowned. "How about the research data?"

Andrew shrugged. "Haven't got to that yet."

"Do it now."

"What?" The young captain stared at the former security guard, his eyebrows raised. Then he slapped his forehead. "Of course! Toni, would you and Nzinga..."

"We're on it."

"Look for..."

"I know. Recent uploads and downloads of key data."

They bombed into the database, first shutting all the former employees out of everything. Then they cycled back, allowing each one access to personal information once they had run it through a rudimentary screen for scientific words, phrases, and images.

While they worked, the meeting started. Even using *Diablo's* Otherwhere communication, there was a five-minute delay with the ambassador and three minutes with *NightHawk*, so nothing happened quickly.

Once everyone was up to speed on everyone else's progress, Pretoro took command. "This is how it looks to me. I don't think we can use that base for its intended purpose. Morissa will probably agree. I understand your concern about putting these barwolves back into the regular community, and the need to study them. But if the race's widespread knowledge of Chakka is any indication, it is impossible to control information in this society. This also leads us towards a verdict of intelligence. Let's start moving ahead on ideas for creating a preserve on the base island. Protection of the base itself is paramount.

"I also agree that these specimens...individuals, I should say...would be valuable as research subjects, as long as we can be sure it is voluntary. But to ask them to stay in this place that has been such a torture for them would be horrible, and would probably skew your data all over the place.

"The base is to be mothballed. Take anything that seems useful to your research. Leave the base in operating condition, running at minimum power." He grinned. "In the Outback we don't waste anything. Somebody, someday, might find a use for the place.

"I'll send Major Bykov a new set of orders detailing the shut-down procedures. He will be given command of the base when Morissa and Andrew leave." A sly look crossed his face. "That should keep everyone happy. Dr. Goodall, most of these decisions concern the accuracy and impartiality of your research. Comments?"

Eyes turned towards Morissa. "The more I think about it, the less I want to deal with the contaminated individuals right now. My original assignment was to assess the barwolf society as it stands. With the time pressures involved, I should continue that process. Once my initial decision is made, then I assume I will be allowed to move to the next stage of the research: to discover the potential for future interaction with Humanity."

They waited, and soon a new transmission came in from the embassy. "Good. We'll proceed on those parameters. The message I just got from Captain O'Rourke will be useful in your setup procedures. I'm turning this situation over to her for reasons you'll soon understand. Well done, team. Pretoro out."

Almost immediately Natalia appeared on the screen. "I'm agreeing with all of it. The only change is that someone has to be responsible for settling the new preserve. It seems to me we have two staff with organic augments and one auguar, all with their assignments completed. Alfino and I will hash out a chain of command that allows you independent authority over that part of the operation, assuming close cooperation with Morissa. We can't put you under her command, but I don't have to emphasize the importance of her research." She glanced at something offscreen. "Now, I have more important things to do at the moment other than to give useless advice to people that don't need it." Her body lurched, and she reached out to steady the coffee cup on the desk in front of her. "I'll drop in once I have this little wrinkle ironed out."

She signed off, leaving Toni and Andrew staring at each other.

He shook his head. "Do you know how abrupt a course change it takes to overpower *NightHawk's* new inertial system?"

Toni shrugged. "About 3 Gs?"

"It seems the Barnard System isn't quite pacified yet."

They turned to Morissa, who nodded. "Official orders will come later. Here and now we work it out ourselves." She grinned. "Just like we always do in the Outback."

She turned to Jackson. "I'm not sure who gives you orders, but you're way ahead of us on the data security situation. Dr. Flagstaff was pushing me hard about his research results. He's still hoping to profit from them somehow, flawed and inconclusive as they are."

The security man nodded. "If I was him, I'd already have a backup stored somewhere personal. If he wasn't that smart, his next move would be to download what he can onto portable media."

Toni shook her head. "We checked his logs first. He hasn't moved any documents of any size at all since we took over. Now that we have time, we'll check much closer and we'll take the same precautions with all the staff." She grinned. "What better carrier than someone innocuous like the cook?" She turned to Jackson. "What else is on your mind? Now that the action is over, I'm starting to think further down the road."

"Me too. I questioned the guards. There's a scheduled radio contact with their home base in two days. They don't know where the base is; it's probably mobile. We won't be able to fool anyone, so at that point the leaders of this operation will know they've been busted. What will they do then, and how will we prepare for it?"

Toni shrugged. "First option is they bust in and take it all back."

"I've already got Major Bykov drilling his men on the base's defences."

"They have some?"

"Not much. We'll be counting on our ships to defend us. But don't we have to send the IPC home pretty quick?"

Andrew nodded. "If we only have two days, we should get them out of here now. It's pretty much a 24-hour turnaround to the Tree Planet. They could get back, deliver the next twenty and be out of here with the last ten before that radio contact even happens."

Morissa shook her head. "But we have no facilities ready for them. We can't just turn them loose. What if they decide to trash our camp?"

They were interrupted by a map that appeared on the forward view screens and in their augments.

"What's this, *Diablo?*"

Possible solution, sir.

"Orient us, please."

A glowing point appeared on a landmass near the bottom of the map.

That is the north end of the island the base is on. This archipelago is well-spaced, and several islands are roughly the size of a standard barwolf hunting territory.

"You're a genius, *Diablo.*"

Thank you, sir.

Toni gazed at the map. "If only we knew how far they can swim."

Morissa nodded. "They've surprised us by loving the water already, but they have a body density of 1.15. If they're changing islands, they'll have to walk."

Andrew shook his head. "It's a chance we'll have to take. There's plenty of food left in the freezers here. We dump each group off wherever they want with a supply of food and leave the rest at camp. The shuttles can take over the feeding and monitoring from there. It's only temporary."

Morissa stood. "I'll have to go. I'm no use here anyway, and I can coordinate better from camp."

Andrew grinned. "Where there's better shower facilities."

She aimed a swat somewhere near his head, smiling. "Who's coming with me?"

Toni stood as well. "Andrew and *Diablo* need to stay here in case of a military situation. Nzinga and I are best onship with the first load. In fact…" she glanced down at the brindle barwolf, lying in Chakka's accel couch.

"What?"

"I think you'll have much less chance of trouble with the second group if we have a sure way of telling them what happens when they get home."

"You're going to take the Brindle and send it back?" Andrew looked thoughtful. "It's already wandering all over the place and hasn't caused any trouble yet." He slapped his hands on the arm of his couch. "Right. We'll send two of the marines to man the defences on the IPC and guard the prisoners, and Achmed or Alison can fly wingman in case of trouble. Harriers have superior sensors, so you should be able to spot any trouble at long range. They can drop you off on those islands, take Morissa and Toni to camp, and come right back." His speech quickened and his hands flashed. "Twenty more in the next trip, and the rest of us can handle the ten extras among us. The IPC won't even have to make a third trip. The whole lot of us can be clear of here in 48 hours."

Toni was trying to keep up. "Who's going to look after the second load of barwolves? You're not going to leave the pilot of the IPC by himself?"

Jackson raised a finger. "I'm not sure, but it's possible, if everything is going well and we can work something out, the Brindle and I might be able to handle it."

"You think so?" Andrew shook his head. "What if it makes a gestalt and takes over the ship?"

"And does what? The moment anything goes wrong we lock ourselves in the cockpit and gas them."

"I suppose. I don't like it much, so let's save that for a last-ditch effort."

The big man shrugged. "Fair enough. I'm not exactly enthused, but I thought I'd offer."

"We appreciate it." The captain looked around. "any other ideas?" After a short silence he nodded. "Then let's get moving."

As Toni was leaving he held her back. "You'll be an hour or so?"

"At least."

"Can I borrow Nzinga? I'm going on a data hunt, and I could use the backup. Good practice for her, as well."

Image: auguar and Chakka's Cub working together. Emotion: eager desire to please.

The two humans grinned at each other. Nzinga curled up on the left-hand accel couch, Andrew took the captain's position, and they were both deep in gestalt before Toni got out the door.

Now that she had such little time to get everything done, Toni went into not-quite-panic mode, moving quickly, checking off items on her mental list and trying desperately not to miss something obvious. She consulted with Bill and had two of the Marines go EV to attach several crates of frozen *alces barnardus* meat to the equipment racks on the outside of the IPC's hull. As long as they were kept out of the direct sunlight, they would stay frozen.

Andrew was still busy with his task, so Toni had *Diablo* move off the airlock and had the IPC lock on. Soon the four scientists were meekly following her into the carrier. They had decided to split the group in half, and the cook, unsure of his next employment, was happy to stay on and keep working. The security officers and the maintenance man had similar hopes of switching allegiance, so they were willing to stay and do the grunt work and assist with their knowledge of the working of the base.

Once everything was packed, she contacted Andrew. *Interplanetary Personnel Carrier Barnard 16 ready for launch, sir. We seem to be missing a crew member.*

There was a pause, and then Andrew answered. *Just a moment...okay...got it. Let's get out of here, Pumpkin.*

Any luck?

The two of them appeared in the airlock. "Did the best we could." He handed Toni her satchel of personal belongings, and Nzinga bounded aboard the IPC. Toni and Andrew stood a moment, staring at each other. Then he smiled, gave his usual perfect salute, and stepped back. She saluted as well and sent the order to close the hatch.

The IPC lifted away slowly, and the pilot began a gradually increasing acceleration. Despite this caution, Toni noticed an immediate rise in emotion in their passengers.

Emotion: question?

Image: barwolves in cages, mashed against the bars under heavy acceleration.

Emotion: negation. Image: Barwolves resting against padded wall of room as velocity increased.

"What's going on?" Morissa was sitting in the copilot's couch, looking at the monitors.

"They remember a bad time on the trip out. Nobody took the acceleration into account. We've reassured them, and they're settling."

"Oh, yes. Look at them now."

As soon as the thrust became strong enough that the rear wall of the room was "down," the anxiety began to drop off. An understandable level of excitement kept up throughout the flight, but nothing to worry about. Toni reached down and rubbed at the brown shoulder beside her.

Emotion: satisfaction.

Emotion: satisfaction.

Emotion: Pride and satisfaction.

"Yes, Nzinga. We did a good job."

All went well for several hours, but then the pilot glanced over at Toni. "Incoming message, ma'am. The *NightHawk*."

"Put it up."

Captain O'Rourke came on the viewscreen. "Hello, everyone. I hope you're making progress, because our timeline just got changed. One of the shuttles caught a kidnapper on the ground. Since all our military backup was busy, they handled it themselves." She grinned. "They all snuck up on the other shuttle and pounced on him from four directions. I gather it was some very pretty piloting. They caught the trappers outside their vehicle, and their hunting rifles weren't up to penetrating a shuttle hull, so the perps surrendered pretty quickly. Of course, not before they made a call to their masters. So our enemy knows something it up. I'd expect a visit from them any time, Andrew. May I assume our IPC is enroute with the first contingent of settlers?"

A view of Andrew showed up on the other screen. "Yes, ma'am. Toni and the scientists are about halfway home with Lieutenant Rowell as escort. Any backup expected from anywhere?"

After a couple of minutes pause the answer came back. "None for the next ten or twelve hours. Captain Worthing has a couple of his boys headed your way with enough spare tanks to get there, but they'd better not have to fight for very long."

Andrew's face blanked for a moment as he calculated. "If they're coming in from SC1 in the Inner Belt, they could swing by and escort the IPC back out."

When Natalia's image became active again she, too was in her gestalt. She looked up. "That's perfect. I'll put up a virtual map of the area, and *NightHawk* and *Diablo* can update it as the data arrives."

The pilot raised his eyebrows and motioned towards the com system, but Toni shook her head. "We don't have access to their com, and they're way out of augment range. At least you'll have company on your way back out."

"Can't complain about that, ma'am. Will they be those old Junkers 73B's?"

She grinned. "Out here something as recent as a 73B is pretty new. All you care about is that they go a lot faster than you do, so they'll have no trouble catching up. I assume the whole flotilla will be making the return journey together, so you'll have plenty of powerful company." She glanced at him. "You're from the *Nebraska*. How did you end up out here?"

"I was on my way back from a delivery, and it turned out I was the nearest ship of the right configuration. Bit of a lark, really. Until Lady Luck took a swing at my head." He frowned. "Are we looking at real action, here?"

She shrugged. "No idea. The guys who kidnapped these barwolves have enough money to set up the operation, but we don't know anything about them. Unless our show of force scares them away, I guess we're about to have a learning experience." She made a quick check with Lieutenant Rowell, who had heard the whole conversation and was ready for action.

Then Toni left her seat and went to check on the marines, whom she found going over their weapons. "How do they look?"

Sergeant Zuyeva, a stocky woman with a Slavic look, nodded judiciously. "The 50-calibre machine guns on the turrets are good equipment, ma'am. Plenty of boost and good accuracy." She hefted her Standard Issue Glock. "If anyone gets past them and tries to board, they won't get far."

She grinned. "Not with anti-personnel rounds in the chamber."

"You've used one of these?"

"Only to try it out. Commandos usually use a longer-range, lower-rate weapon like the Colt 218."

She glanced at the other Marine, a hulking Weapons Specialist named Fraser, but he merely nodded and went back to oiling his weapon.

"Midpoint flip in about twenty minutes, guys. It'll be a slow one because of our passengers."

Zuyeva grinned. "I've seen those teeth. Whatever keeps 'em happy, ma'am."

Satisfied, she continued her rounds. Both cabins of barwolves were stable and relatively calm. She made a perfunctory visit to the scientists but stayed only long enough to assure herself that they were healthy. The less she heard from Dr. Flagstaff the better.

She returned to the cockpit. "All right, Mulloy. This is going to be the gentlest flip you've ever done. You have twenty wild barwolves that are going to be experiencing free fall for the second time., and I doubt the first time was fun. Let's slide them into it gently and take them out the same way."

"Aye, ma'am. Gentle is the word. Easing acceleration now."

The whine of the engines spooled slowly down to silence. As gravity disappeared, the feeling of the barwolf gestalt hesitated, then began to grow.

Feeling: anxiety, fear, puzzlement.

"Come on, Nzinga. We have to calm them."

Feeling: joy, pleasure.

Feeling: question?

Image: Queen Nzinga, soaring high above her subjects. Feeling: joy, freedom.

Feeling: awe

Feeling: Invitation.

Feeling: hesitant acceptance, timid hesitance, relief, pleasure, freedom. JOY!

Morissa was fairly bouncing in her accel couch. "Look at them, Toni. Have you ever seen anything like it?

Toni accessed the cameras. The barwolves were leaping and cavorting in their gravityless room, bouncing off each other, the walls, the ceiling. She could hear the crashing of armour plates all the way up in the cockpit.

"Mulloy, take it easy, but get us some gravity in there as soon as is humanly possible. Otherwise they're gonna trash the place."

"Acceleration in 5...4, 3, 2, 1, Go."

The engines whined up the scale and gradually the weight returned.

Emotion: disappointment, sadness. Memory: flying! Great joy! Emotion: Awe and reverence.

Toni checked the viewscreen. The cameras were still running in both rooms, one of them blurred by a cracked lens. From what she could see, there was superficial damage to all surfaces. One of the nul-G toilets was leaking a fine spray of water, but otherwise all was calm.

Mulloy was shaking his head. "Never seen the like, ma'am."

"Can you think of any way to make it easier next time?"

He shook his head. "That was about as smooth as I can do it."

"Then we have to send our brindled friend back to coach the next batch through. At least you'll know to split the difference between quick and soft."

"Do my best, ma'am."

"Well, back to accel as she goes, Pilot. I'm going in to play plumber."

They kept close watch on the barwolves for the rest of the journey, but both packs had settled more than Toni had ever seen. Curious, she and Nzinga slid into the gestalt the Brindle was connected to.

Many interconnected images: floating, flying, bouncing. Emotions: freedom, joy.

Toni recorded a sample of the sensations in her augment, then pulled Nzinga free before they were both caught up in the wonderful ecstasy of the gestalt.

"Morissa, you should see this. It's some sort of emotion-sharing ritual. Almost religious."

The scientist looked at the viewscreens, puzzled. "What? There's nothing happening."

"Oh. I guess it only shows up on the augment. Girl, you definitely need an upgrading."

"I suppose I do."

* * *

As the shuttle approached the Tree Planet, Toni stopped patrolling and went back to the cockpit. "Next challenge, Mulloy. We have two tonnes of frozen moosey meat on the outer hull. If we barbecue it on entry, you'll have gravy stains on your hull and a mess to clean up once we've fed our customers."

"Let me guess. You want me to bring her in just fast enough to defrost dinner."

She regarded him. "Geez, and here I always thought pilots were drawn from the flunkees from cooking school."

He shrugged. "Bound to be a few incongruities slip through the nets, ma'am."

"I refuse to be amazed at your vocabulary. Just get us on the ground before the steak is well done."

"As you wish, ma'am. Take…" his eyes blanked as he accessed his augment, "…an extra 1.5 hours and 1,068 litres of fuel."

"May I assume we have enough in the tanks?"

"4,399 litres, ma'am."

"I'm counting on you to tell me if that's a reasonable cushion."

He shrugged again. "I am the pilot, ma'am. It's what I do."

"Your attitude fills me with confidence. Proceed on your own course, Pilot."

"One large moosey steak, medium rare, coming up, ma'am."

* * *

It wasn't quite that simple, because their orders were to rid themselves of their human passengers before they dealt with the barwolves. As Morissa put it, there was no need to give Flagstaff any more fuel for his pretense that he knew what was going on, and she had work to catch up on.

So, it took four more valuable hours before they set down on the first containment island. Toni and Nzinga determined, with the help of the Brindle, that the two separate groups wished to maintain their packs. Unsure of what awaited them, they landed at an appropriate clearing near a water source, opened the airlock, set down the gangplank, and opened the closest stateroom door.

179

An avalanche of barwolves bashed their way along the main corridor of the IPC and out the airlock. When they reached the soil of their native planet, their gestalt exploded with uncontained emotion. Toni had to restrain herself from clapping her hands over her ears; it would have done no good, because the volume was all in her head. The barwolves burst away in all directions, running and leaping in their awkward way. Some rubbed their shoulders against the ground like dogs, while others leaped high and spun in the air.

After a further moment of madness, the barwolves all disappeared into the bush, their gestalt dwindling as they separated.

Toni glanced at the two marines, shrugged, and followed down the gangplank at a more sedate pace. They made short work of opening one of the meat containers and dumping the food out, spreading it around on the turf.

Jacobs to Mulloy.

Aye, ma'am.

Compliments to the chef. Medium rare as ordered.

All part of the service, ma'am.

Okay, everyone. Happy landing is over. Let's get out of here and do it all again. This time, I'm going to get better video.

They approached the second dropoff point with only ten barwolves and the Brindle onboard. It was a pleasant island, similar to the others, with clumps of the fan-limbed trees and large open tracts of grass and brush. A tall, rocky tor dominated the scene, and they decided on a landing spot near a spring that revealed itself by the show of lush greenery sweeping away from the base of the hill.

Having lived through the experience once already, Toni was determined to get accurate video coverage of their passengers' first moments of freedom. It would be good data for Morissa's study, but when it came right down to it, Toni had never in her life experienced such an outpouring of joy, and she wanted to fully appreciate it.

This was the initial pack she had led into their room at the lab, and their cohesiveness and maturity as a group showed it. Her first, favourite trio led the way, moving with the dignity afforded by their older member. Of course, the young one was dancing with anticipation, but the solemnity of the seniors held sway. Following close behind came the new trio, each inching forward in anticipation, then holding back with anxious looks at the others to see how they were taking this experience.

Once their hooves touched the soil, however, the restraint broke down. The youngest member of the first trio launched into its usual tear, and the others seemed to shrug their heavy shoulders and join in. Soon the clearing was a riot of moving bodies, indulging in their shoulder-scraping rituals with each other and with members of the pack at large.

The Brindle stood at the head of the gangway and watched the goings-on with dignity.

Image: Brindle joining in the fun. Emotion: question?

Image: Brindle standing with Pride Leader and Nzinga

Toni gave the barwolf a shove. "Get down there and enjoy yourself. You know you want to."

The barwolf responded with an incomprehensible mixture of images and emotions and launched itself into the melée.

Toni glanced at the two marines, standing armed and ready. "Don't think you need the hardware, guys. Time to serve dinner."

They opened another food container and laid the meat out as they had before. Immediately the striped barwolf ceased its cavorting and trotted over. It slashed off a small portion of food, picked it up and trotted back into the IPC. A moment later it reappeared in the hatchway.

The barwolf gestalt burst into action, but the messages came too fast to follow. All the barwolves stopped and faced the space fighter. Then they all lowered their bodies to the ground, making a symbolic gesture with one hoof. The Brindle gave some kind of signal and turned, looking up at Toni.

Emotion: satisfaction.

181

Toni nodded and stepped into the airlock, Nzinga and the Brindle following. The Marines collected their weaponry and they all entered the ship and headed for home. There, the pilot left them and he and Brindle headed offplanet again.

19.   ΛTTΛCK

After the excitement of the last week, the base was a distinct letdown. Of the mysterious enemy there was no sign. The prisoners were housed, Morissa went to work on the latest research data, and Toni and Nzinga had little to do. The shuttles dropped off food at the containment islands on their way to and from their assignments and reported normal activity. Lacking transportation or an emergency serious enough to commandeer any, the pair was confined to the camp.

Which gave Toni the leisure to look around.

What she noticed was that Alison Rowell had similar problems. She seemed to be moving around a great deal, but not really doing anything. In fact, should anyone notice, it was possible to conclude that she was doing a lot of things to disguise the fact that something else was going on.

Toni strolled over to Morissa's office. "Got a moment?"

The scientist glanced at the viewscreen. "Doesn't hurt to take a break."

"In other words, no. Just a simple question. Have you noticed Lieutenant Rowell?"

"Not particularly. Why?"

Toni shrugged. "I don't know. Just something bothering me."

Morissa interlaced her fingers. "We haven't gone too far wrong by relying on your hunches. What do you think it is?"

"Well...it's either a letdown from all the action last week, or Alison is up to something." She's been out on patrol twice today, both times without explanation. Not that she has to explain, it's just that this time she didn't."

"Have you checked her radio traffic?"

"I don't really have the authority to do that."

"I'm not sure I do either. Let's take the Andrew approach."

"If they don't tell you that you can't...?"

"That's it." She rose. "I feel the need to stretch my legs."

They strolled across the camp, heading coincidentally for the radio room. Once there, Morissa stuck her head in the door. "Say, Jasper, I need to make a high-security call. Can you give me a moment?"

"Sure thing, ma'am. Do you want me to set it up?"

"No, if I have any trouble, I have Nzinga to make it all work."

He grinned. "Fine with me, ma'am. See you in fifteen?"

"Fifteen will be fine."

As soon as the man was out of sight, Toni took his chair, and she and Nzinga entered the logs. It took much less than fifteen minutes, and they were forced to sit and stew for the rest of the time until the operator returned, chewing happily on a fresh pastry the cook had given him.

As soon as they were out in the middle of the yard, Morissa put a hand on Toni's arm. "What did you get?"

"Nothing and everything. She's made several calls, one from her ship and three from here. No idea where, but offplanet for sure. Call signs and channels scrambled by sophisticated equipment."

"What does that mean?"

"Basically nothing. They could be perfectly legitimate. I just don't know..."

A blast on the com interrupted her. "Lieutenant Jacobs, report to radio room."

They shared a glance, then ran.

"What's up, Jasper?"

"Message from Shuttle 3. They touched down at the first island. No barwolves present, ma'am."

"What do you mean?"

"According to him, they're gone. They did a low-level sweep with all sensors. No barwolves."

"What about the second island?"

"He didn't say, ma'am."

184

"Page Lieutenant Rowell and get her to her ship. Call the ground crews and have them prep it for immediate departure."

She sprinted for her rooms. "Come on, Nzinga. We're going to need our space armour."

They suited up and got to the Harrier just as Rowell was arriving, suited as well. She didn't seem surprised, just started up the ladder to the airlock. "We'll talk once we get moving."

It seemed a strange turn of phrase, but Toni didn't react, just followed.

They improvised an accel couch for Nzinga and soon were blasting off. Once they were settled at a G-and-a-half acceleration, Toni felt it was time for the truth. "Do you know where we're going?"

Alison pounded on the arm of her couch with an armoured fist. "Oh, yes, I know. Damn them! Damn them!"

"Damn who?"

The pilot sighed deeply and calmed herself. "I've got an admission to make."

"I thought you might."

Rowell shot her a glance. "I should have known I wasn't putting anything over. You called it from the get-go."

"I did?"

"Yes. That first meeting we had at the Embassy. You were right. I'm a Space Arm pilot with ties to the interplanetaries. I sincerely believe that a strong economy pays for everything we do."

"And how is that working out?"

"Most of the time it's no problem. The Space Arm doesn't worry about anyone's political sympathies."

"But it didn't stay that way."

"Of course not. My political allies started to put pressure on me. They just wanted information. Nothing classified, mind you. Nothing illegal. Just the considered opinion of someone out here where the ordnance is live. I was flattered and did the best I could within the parameters of my Space Arm oath."

185

"And since I know where that went, can we skip to the present situation?"

"A friend introduced me to someone who had a project where I could be of use. I had no idea what the project was. That was the real reason I was headed out to the lab. Jackson needing a ride was just a good excuse. All they wanted to know was whether the lab had been compromised. I wasn't sure that was any of their business, but since they owned the lab, I thought perhaps they had a right to know. Anyway, once I got out there and realized the scope of the atrocity, I knew I had a problem."

"You tried to let them down easy."

"How did you know that?"

"Commando training these days isn't all fighting and shooting. We take a lot of classes with the spies and counter-terrorists."

"Yeah, well, they said that was fine. They didn't want to blow my cover. Well, that really set me off. I didn't consider myself under any kind of cover. So, I didn't call back. It didn't matter."

"What? Did they put a tail on you?"

"I don't know. When this is over I'll have to check all my belongings. But they knew we came back, and they've been monitoring your vessels, and when the shuttles changed their usual courses back and forth…"

"They put two and two together."

"Exactly. I called them and asked them what was going on, and they offered me a position. They told me their plans. Someone smarter than Dr. Flagstaff has been reading his data. They know that twenty is a good number for a gestalt, and they're going to work on that. They also have plans to develop the planet for real estate the moment the barwolves are declared non-intelligent."

Alison turned in her seat to stare at Toni. "I don't know how they think they can influence that decision, and that makes me worried for Morissa. That's when I knew I'd reached the end of the line. I told them I'd think about it. I was going to wait until Andrew got back and tell you all, put you on your guard. I guess they thought of that, too. They've already made their move. I've plotted a course over the second island, but we know what we'll

186

find. They've picked up all twenty barwolves, and they're hotfooting it out of the system as we speak."

"But you already have a plan?"

"We shouldn't have too much trouble catching them. They're only using one shuttle, and I assume they had to load their victims one by one into the holding area of the mothership."

"What do you know about their mothership?"

"One of the members of the organization has a big cruiser. Sort of a cross between a yacht and a cargo ship. He's been living on it. I imagine that's what they'll be using."

"You're talking about something the size of *NightHawk* or larger. Well armed?"

"Some weapons, for sure."

"We don't have much chance with just a Harrier, and we can't exactly blow them out of the sky with twenty hostages aboard. We've got a destroyer in the area...." she accessed her augment. "Yes, the *Devonshire* is...a week away. No help there. We'll contact her captain, but he won't be able to do anything but sit on the com during the action and pick up the pieces if it all goes sideways. Any ideas?"

"I haven't figured out what to do, yet. But I can catch them and get us aboard. All have to do is offer to join up. They'll be ecstatic to get me plus my ship. I was sort of hoping..."

"That between us we could come up with something before we get there. Fair enough. Have you found them yet?"

Rowell nodded to a blip on the forward viewscreen. "Coming up in about an hour and a half. Good thing. I don't have enough fuel to run at this power level for any longer and still make it home."

"All right. Let's get to planning."

It was a short meeting, because there was little to plan. Alison contacted Captain Jones for a discussion, but he could contribute little.

"The only weakness I can see in your approach is treating this like a hostage situation. If you do so, and then the barwolves are

187

declared non-intelligent, you will have overstepped serious boundaries. Not a great career move."

Rowell glanced at Toni, then shrugged. "But if I don't act, and they are declared intelligent, I will have doomed twenty sapient entities to torture and enslavement. How can I worry about my career with that as the alternative? Besides, none of us on the project have any doubt of the verdict. Especially what we've seen the past week."

"Well, Lieutenant, you know the situation best, so it's your call. I wouldn't dream of interfering. We're here for moral support, if nothing else. Good luck."

"Thank you, sir." She signed off and glanced at Toni. "Anything to add?"

Toni shrugged. "You've made your choice. Let's make sure it comes out the way we planned it."

The pilot wiggled her fingers along the control surfaces of her chair and squirmed into a more comfortable position. "Bring 'em on. We're ready."

Soon they were approaching the enemy ship. Built for long-term residency, it was basically a squat cylinder made of four counter-rotating habitation rings. The aft section looked modular, with whatever engines the owner wanted installed there. At the moment it was cruising above the Tree Planet's asteroid rings, waiting for Alison to board before it headed out to wherever its owners planned to hide next.

"They've got good shielding. Nzinga can't read much."

Rowell frowned. "What do we do?"

Toni gave a grim smile. "What commandos do best. Break in and take over. Once we're inside, I'll demand surrender. I'll kill as many as necessary. If I have to, I'll turn the barwolves loose and let them finish the job."

"And I stay on my ship, engines on standby, minimum docking contact."

"Your inner airlock hatch closed and the outer one open. If I turn the barwolves loose, we don't know what will happen.

188

We're in space armour, so you can pull away as long as we're in the outer lock or attached to your ship."

Alison's face paled, but she nodded and turned back to her ship's controls. "Okay. Headed for a landing."

The Harrier's main hatch was in its belly, and they dropped in over the other ship's airlock just like a vertical ground landing. Soon the seals were tight, and Toni and Nzinga were waiting to dive through the moment the hatch opened.

This was the key point. It all depended on how much the enemy trusted Alison. She stood in the centre of the airlock, anchored by the Harrier's rudimentary grav plates, waiting.

Toni used their gestalt to watch Alison's view through the door as it slid aside. Only two men stood there, weapons holstered on their hips.

The tall one on the left is the leader.

Thanks, Alison. I'll take it from here in three, two, one, Go!

The pilot dove back to the left and Toni and Nzinga blasted in from top and bottom. The commando flattened the right-hand man with the butt of her rifle and backed the leader up against the wall with the muzzle of her weapon. Meanwhile, the auguar was working her way into the ship's systems, opening every door she could find.

Image: barwolves in one large, bare room.

Image: barwolf room closed, all other doors open.

Emotion: agreement.

Toni opened her external com. "Stand your men down."

The leader held his hands clear, his eyes shooting from side to side. "What do you want?"

"Surrender your ship to Space Arm officials. You may consider yourself under arrest."

Image: heat signatures creeping down corridors.

Toni reversed her rifle and slammed the butt into the man's stomach, turning to face her attackers. They came from both directions, five or six each way, all with handguns. She backed into the cross-corridor, muzzle sweeping left and right.

The man on the floor moaned and tried to rise. "Kill them. Kill them all."

As the men's pistols came up, Toni started firing. Without prompting, Nzinga opened the final door.

A rush of barwolves filled the corridor from the aft part of the ship, overwhelming the enemy in that hallway. A torrent of augment power filled Toni's head. Blinded by multiple visions, she sprayed the forward tunnel with anti-personnel rounds. Then the gestalt became too much for her. It invaded her brain, and her consciousness ebbed…

…it was the same old nightmare: the screaming kitten, trailing blood as the boys threw it back and forth. Her panic and anger as she attacked them, to be thrown viciously to the pavement, where she lay sobbing. She especially remembered the nasty grin of the gang leader as he tossed the kitten's torn body on her chest and turned away…

…but this time she had her gun. She raised the old reliable Colt and fired, 50-calibre low-velocity anti-personnel rounds spraying the enemy. A whole pride of cats surrounded her, their huge teeth tearing into the bodies, throwing men like dolls. The kitten, instead of dying in her arms, jumped free and led the charge, her agile mind opening doors and closing down weapons systems.

From then on it was just the blur of a battle seen through many eyes, the instant knowledge of every move: what to do, where to go, how to arrange her squad. Twice she felt the agony of death: the cold blankness in her mind as she lost one of her pride, but the gestalt closed over the wound and attacked more fiercely. Screaming human faces confronted her and were swept away. Nzinga led them through the ship, pointing out each enemy, her augment burning a path through the electronics.

Then, finally, everything went still. Toni came to her senses with hard bodies surrounding her, holding her up, cushioning her mind against the horror of the battle. Nzinga was there, anxiously rubbing against her armour. Then the gestalt faded and she slipped deeper into soft, inviting darkness.

Toni. Toni, this is Andrew. Are you there? What's happening?

...Andrew...?

Toni, are you all right? There was an incredible spike on the augment. Even the pilots could feel it. We're on track to be there in an hour. What's your status? Are you captured? Injured? Toni? Answer, please.

...Andrew.

Image: Nzinga and Andrew talking.

Nzinga? What's wrong?

Image: Pride Leader asleep in pile of barwolves.

Emotion: satisfaction, worry.

I'm not getting this, Toni. Nzinga is happy and worried all at once. Are you with the barwolves?

Image: cruiser drifting in space, engines cold.

Okay, I'm getting the same info from Alison, but she's afraid to come on board, because the barwolves are loose. I told her not to risk it if you didn't need her. We'll be there soon. Just hold on.

Emotion: satisfaction.

A rough tongue rasped Toni's face, and Nzinga's purr filled her ears. It almost made up for the great emptiness she felt. Time seemed to disappear, as one moment she was alone with the barwolves and Nzinga and all the dead men, and the next she was somehow in a bunk on *Diablo,* but her auguar was...*where?*

Image: Nzinga cuddled close to Pride Leader, licking her face.

Then the barwolves faded from her mind, and she felt as alone as she had ever been in her life. "No...no...! Bring them back..."

Andrew was there, holding her hand, his palm on her forehead. "You're okay, Toni."

"No, no, you can't take them away. Bring them back...bring them back. Please!" She was sobbing like a child.

"Okay, okay, calm down. We'll go back and get them."

Diablo, reverse course.

And then it all faded again.

* * *

When she regained consciousness, Andrew was there, still holding her hand, his other palm on her forehead. She read the lines on his face. *He's too young to have those lines.* She had to get up.

"No, no, everything's all right. Stay there."

"I will not! If everything was all right you wouldn't look so worried. What's gone wrong this time?"

"You. You're what's gone wrong. You've been out for four hours, and so deep in your augment that you were inaccessible. I've been going out of my mind."

"Well, I'm accessible now, and we've got a whole bunch of mess to clean up. Tell me what happened and let me out of here."

"Okay. If I tell you what happened, will you calm down?"

"If you'd stop treating me like a child...!"

"I'm treating you like an invalid who has been through an experience no other human has undergone. I know I'm supposed to be the expert on augments, but this is above my pay grade."

"Prime. You don't know what's going on. Trust me. I'm fine. Now, tell me what happened."

"All right. First, you and the barwolves went into full gestalt. Just like back at the underground lab, but huge. We were two hours away, and we could still feel it."

"I figured that much." She cringed at the images that evoked. "Then the barwolves killed the crew of the cruiser... no." She straightened her back. "<u>We</u> killed the crew of the cruiser. In fact, I killed them. We were in gestalt, and I was leading it, and I took my cadre in and slaughtered those men, killed them just like that massacre back on the Tree Planet."

He nodded. "Something like that, but I don't think you can take all the credit. I'm sorry, but you were unconscious for a long time, and I was really worried about you, so I took some liberties I wasn't really supposed to without your permission. You weren't in any state to give it." He took her hand. "I hope you don't mind. I was really worried."

She frowned. "What do you mean?"

"I accessed your augment records."

"Oh. And what did you find?"

"Just what I told you. Marissa is going to be ecstatic. You just put the two biggest parts of the barwolf puzzle together. You formed a full gestalt and went into a controlled killing frenzy. It was totally frightening, and that's one bit of data that will go into full security lockdown for just about ever. We don't want anybody in the outside universe to know what they're capable of."

"Good little soldiers, are we?"

"No pain, no fear, just the burning desire to tear the enemy to shreds."

"We wouldn't want that to get out in certain circles."

He shrugged. "With your specific data as backup, Morissa is busy redefining the concept of intelligence to include group minds, which makes the conclusion of her study rather simple. If you put five barwolves in a room with Nzinga, she'd have them doing calculus in about three days. Or destroying the security programming and creating their own mathematics. That's more her style."

"Nzinga." She sat up. "Nzinga! Where is she?" She looked around the room. "I thought she was here. I could feel her the whole time." She started to climb off bed. "Where is she?"

Andrew's hands were on her shoulders. "She was here, but now she's back on the cruiser taking care of the barwolves."

"Oh. Where is the cruiser?"

"Travelling as close alongside *Diablo* as two ArIns can pilot."

"I don't understand."

"We don't either, really. When we got to the cruiser we didn't know what to do. You were completely out of it, but Nzinga got you to the airlock, and we brought you on board. The barwolves weren't too happy about that, but we had brought the Brindle with us, and it and Nzinga were able to calm them. There we were, with you in a coma and a spaceship full of vicious barwolves and seventeen dead bodies. The *Devonshire* offered to come over, but by the time they got here, the barwolves would be pretty thirsty. So, we decided to just leave them there until we could send a tug to tow them home.

But the moment we pulled away you went bonkers, and so did they. We had to go back. Nzinga and Brindle kept them under control while we stored the bodies and cleaned up the mess enough that we could get the cruiser under way.

"So here we are, three hours from Tree Planet orbit. The cruiser can't land, so we'll have to ferry the barwolves down in *Diablo*. Having you awake is going to make my life ever so much easier."

She frowned, looking up into his face. "You've had a pretty rough time of it, haven't you?"

He put up his hands and rubbed his face. "I think that would be a safe guess." Then he looked at her. "You were so deep in their gestalt I didn't know if you were ever coming back. I was afraid to stop the gestalt in case you went with it. I thought we'd lost you, Toni."

He was on the verge of tears. *He lost his mother when he was ten years old.* She couldn't help herself. She reached out and pulled him in so his head was against her shoulder. "But you didn't. You held the fort and got me through it. I'll never forget that. Thanks from the bottom of my heart."

His arms went around her and he pulled her tight for a long, sweet time. Gradually, Toni's inner agony began to fade. The bands of tension around her head eased, and her body relaxed against his.

His voice was muffled against her shoulder. "I think we've been here before."

She scoffed. "It's hardly the same."

He pulled back to look into her eyes. "No, it is the same."

"Oh. I see." She felt his arms slacken, and held him tighter. "Then it isn't the same. Not this time. We'll deal with it."

"We will?" He took her upper arms and held her away. "But not the same way as last time."

194

She looked at her fist. "Whatever's appropriate." She gave the ghost of a grin and pulled loose, swinging her legs over the side of the bunk. "Help me get up and let's get organized. I want to see those barwolves on solid ground."

She stood a moment, his arm around her shoulders, hers around his waist. She looked up at him. "I meant that. Thanks."

He shrugged. "You'd do the same for me."

She pushed him away. "Just you make sure I never have to. Come on. Let's go talk to my pride."

"Yeah, and think up what we're going to write in our report of the action."

She shrugged. "That's easy. The barwolves got loose and killed their captors. Nzinga and I calmed the barwolves down once there were no enemies left. You and *Diablo* came rushing in like the cavalry and saved us. End of story."

He grinned. "Sounds more like a beginning."

20.   NEW ASSIGNMENT

The following week one of the Harrier pilots took Jackson back to the embassy with Morissa along to receive her new implant. The ship returned without her, because she was staying for "further meetings." The members of the rescue team were afforded a much-deserved holiday, and occupied themselves by creating a bathing area, complete with changing rooms and a barbeque, on the small bay closest to the base.

It was pleasant to loll around in the sunlight and swim in the warm waters, but Toni was careful not to spend too much time with Andrew. If he was puzzled by her approach, he didn't say anything about it, merely amused himself by teaching Nzinga how to swim.

Still, Toni felt a surge of anticipation when word went around that *NightHawk* was enroute to bring Morissa home. Idle speculation could only conclude that it was no coincidence. As the scout ship's arrival time approached, a quiet anticipation grew in the base.

When *NightHawk* pulled into orbit around the Arborea, Captain O'Rourke sent an invitation to the leaders of the Research Centre to visit. "Takes less fuel for Andrew to bring all of you up here, and then he can take Morissa back down."

Toni grinned at Andrew after they signed off. "And it gets us meeting on her home territory. Wonder what's up?"

"I'm not worried. If she was mad at me, I'd know."

Toni opened her augment. *Alison. Want to take a little jaunt?*

Emotion: question?

We're invited for tea on NightHawk. Coming?

Emotion: agreement. Emotion: question?

As soon as we can. Diablo's warming her engines as we speak.

The pilot waited until she was within speaking distance on the landing field. "What's going on, Toni?"

She shrugged. "I'm guessing future plans. We're all invited into a Space-Arm-controlled environment. Puts a different slant on things."

"Maybe they're coming clean with the next phase of the operation."

Toni turned towards the cockpit. "We'll know soon enough."

* * *

As they approached the Scout, *Diablo* put a visual up on the viewscreens. *NightHawk* looked more than a little shopworn. Black streaks shot down her port side from a dark hole that indicated injured PermaSkin.

Andrew took control of the image and zoomed in to the left dorsal area. "Are those bullet holes?"

Toni shook her head. "Too irregular. Shrapnel, I'd say."

The angles of entry and deflection indicate a close detonation of small charge, akin to a Surface-to-Space missile like the old Chinese FN-23.

Andrew chuckled. "She did say she was on important business."

The zoom became live, and a soft "clunk" indicated that they were docked.

Docking clamps secure. Seals tested. Clear for debarking.

The airlock hissed open and they filed through. When Toni had adjusted to the new "down," Jackson stood in front of her. She shook his extended hand. "Didn't expect to see you back so soon."

"Oh, I get around." He grinned. "And don't ask for more, because I don't know, either."

Toni slapped his beefy shoulder. "I wouldn't dream of it."

Jackson turned to greet Alison in what Toni considered a rather friendly fashion. To her surprise, the pilot's usual serene smile warmed in response. They were a strange combination:

her slim, cool, elegance beside his hulking warmth. Toni thought about herself and Andrew and decided to make no judgements.

Then Jackson returned to his normal, busy self and hustled them towards the mess area.

Marissa appeared and swung in beside Toni, who grinned, opening her augment. *Welcome home.*

The scientist took a moment to get into the proper mental frame and engage her augment. *Thank you. Good to be back. Plenty to do.*

New plans from the Higher-Ups?

The scientist took a moment.

Image, slowly forming and clearing: barwolves in gestalt sitting in school room with Nzinga writing equations on viewscreen. My official findings are a rubber stamp, and I have more important objectives. Dr. Pretoro was very firm during our meetings. We're on to level two of the project.

Protecting the barwolves?

And the humans who interface with them. And finding out everything we can about them.

Sounds like right up our alley. Good projection, by the way. Very clear."

My augment is a Standard 10, whatever that means. I'm still getting used to it."

Emotion: warm welcome.

Morissa's face reddened and formed a happy smile. She glanced at Toni, then her shoulders straightened, and she strode into the mess.

Natalia was standing at the head of the main table. She waited for them to be seated, then nodded to Jonny to pass out glasses of wine.

The captain lifted her drink in a silent toast, and they all sipped. "I suppose you're wondering why I have gathered you all together, here."

Andrew snorted. "It can't be to reveal who dunnit, because we're the ones that figured it all out. What's up, Mum? Promotions all 'round? Freighty paying a stockholder dividend?"

Image: large hand slapping Ensign Collingwood behind the ear.

Andrew's expression didn't change. *Image: Ensign Collingwood ducking easily, grinning.*

Morissa's face brightened. "I got that! I saw the whole thing." She turned to Natalia. "You're a mean mother!"

There were chuckles around the table, including from the captain. "Thanks for coming on such short notice. Ambassador Pretoro and Morissa and I have been creating an overview of the coming months and deciding where we are all going to fit."

Toni's heart sank. *Now it comes.*

"Toni, you're looking like your Mum's got measles." Natalia stared at her in concern. "What's up?"

She frowned. "Did I just create a monster? What are we going to do with the barwolves that have attacked and killed humans?"

The captain shook her head. "You didn't create them. The scientists who kidnapped them created a crippled subculture. The idiots who stole our twenty created a further divide." She turned to Morissa. "Your balliwack, I believe."

The scientist nodded. "We have two distinct groups, and they have to be kept separated from each other and segregated from the rest of the population. We need a group to test for interaction with humans, and the last thirty from the lab, damaged as they are, seem the best bet. The original twenty are best kept away from everyone until we have a lot more information about how they will interact with humans, considering their latest experience."

Natalia steepled her fingers. "So, the original twenty continue their idyllic life on the islands. The rest of the lab victims move into our holding area on the north end of Barwolf Base Island. Then we start research, especially on what kind of distance is required to keep them from passing information."

Morissa ticked off points. "And how they pass information, and how many creatures it takes to pass information, and how they deal with trauma."

Toni had a thought. "Is there any way of applying Asimov's Laws to barwolves?"

Andrew shook his head. "His Laws are a substitute for a moral code for mechanical creatures that have no society or history to fall back on. We presume the barwolves have their own moral codes, and we have no right to interfere with them. One of their laws is that too large a group means death. You can't Asimov that."

Jackson nodded. "Alfino and I have been talking on the topic. One of the concepts we're looking at is how we can make a treaty with a group that communicates through augment. I know that sounds weird, but if we can create an agreed-upon set of rules to govern our interspecies interaction, and if they have a way to keep their individual members from breaking the rules..."

Andrew snorted. "And if we could find a way to keep our individuals from breaking ours..."

The captain laid her hands on her desk, her usual sign that she was about to take charge of the meeting again. "And that brings us back to why we're here. Morissa, you consider this to be moving into phase two of the Barwolf program."

The scientist smiled. "As you told me at the time, we were already in it before we started phase one."

"But you're not doing widespread sampling anymore. You won't need so much help on the ground, now."

"I'm new to this sort of thing, but I think more space support?"

"That's right, but it's a small detail in the bigger picture. Here's the overall show." She pulled up a schematic of the two asteroid belts, the mining areas highlighted. "Alfino and Jackson have been delving into the history of mining exploration."

Andrew snapped his fingers. "Gold rush."

"Precisely. California, Barkerville, Yukon, Australia and the Sol Asteroids. The pattern's always the same." She nodded to the big ex-security guard. "Pertinent details, please."

He folded meaty hands on the table. "The usual problems with regulation. Scattered resources, slow transportation, lack of personnel and armament. We're going to have to depend on the locals to do a lot of their own policing, just like they did in gold rush days."

Natalia frowned. "It's going to be the Wild West."

"It's the Outback. That's how Dr. Pretoro sees it, and the Space arm agrees. They're beginning to realize that their five little destroyers are a drop in the bucket. But until more staff and equipment arrive, we're stuck with what we've got."

Andrew stretched his hands in front of him until his knuckles cracked. "So, where does that put us?"

Natalia raised both index fingers to focus their attention. "That's what this meeting is about. The destroyers will do regular patrols. *NightHawk* will stay assigned to the Embassy. We'll continue to do what we have been all along. Putting out brush fires, playing the enforcer for the whole system. But that leaves the Tree Planet relatively unprotected."

Her eyes slid towards Toni. "And we have a small military force here which is already on task, protecting the barwolves and enforcing the quarantine. We plan to bolster that force considerably at first, then increase it slowly as resources and need dictate. But it means a much larger presence on your island, because it's free of natural barwolves, so fair game for human habitation. Most of the new arrivals will be non-military, because we're putting together an administrative hub."

She turned to Alison. "Lieutenant, we'll be increasing your command to a squadron of two small wings. Six Space Arm Harriers and six Outback 73Bs." She smiled. "We have no officers of appropriate rank available, so we're following Outback Rule 1. Experience leads. Admiral Mira agrees that someone with appropriate experience and the rank of Major will be sufficient."

The colour drained from the pilot's already-pale face. "A...squadron? Major?"

"Half size. With all support needed. You'll liaise with Marissa at the Barwolf Centre as you have been, and with whoever leads the civilian contingent. Your task will be to enforce the quarantine in space and support the squad of Marines that will be based here to provide downplanet security."

Toni frowned. "And who will be leading the Marines?"

"Probably Major Bykov. He's available and experienced." The captain focused. "Is that a problem?"

Toni shrugged. "Career officer. He'll either cope or the barwolves will eat him."

"Alison, how do you see it?"

The pilot, too, shrugged. "We get along. I'm not worried. There'll be the usual cross-force command issues that are best worked out on a personal level."

Natalia's face cleared. "And it won't be a problem for you anyway, Toni."

The Commando frowned. "It won't?"

Natalia turned to Andrew. "Tell us about *Diablo's* role."

Her son leaned his elbows on the table. "I'm putting a troubleshooting team together: scientific and security. It'll have to be a small team, so we'll follow Commando practice. Everybody has to qualify two ways."

Natalia nodded. "You can't argue with success. Who are you taking?"

Andrew's eyes slid to Toni. "First thing, I need a head of security. Because it's a Space Arm force, a commissioned officer, but she has to have other skills."

His mother raised her eyebrows. "She?"

Andrew gave his best shrug. "Whattaya say, Toni? You and the Pumpkin in?"

Toni's heart gave a lurch. "Do I have a choice?"

"This is strictly a volunteer situation. Of course you have a choice."

"That's good. When a person is dealing with this lot, she has to be certain she's not being manipulated, cajoled, blackmailed or influenced. You know how it is."

"Um...yeah. I can see that."

"Just so we have that straight."

"Of course, Lieutenant. Whatever you say."

She frowned and pointed a finger at him. "Did I forget to mention 'lied to'?"

The look on his face reminded her that he had just turned seventeen.

"Yes, of course we're coming." She cut off the smile that was forming. "With the usual agreement. You're in charge until danger threatens. Then you do what you're told."

"Right. Until we discover that Freighty has done something to mess up all our plans, at which point we salvage what we can."

"Which will end up with the result that he wanted."

Toni turned to Natalia. "It looks like we have that straight. Let's get to planning."

Natalia extended the invitation for the group to stay overnight so the party could continue. There would be no poker game, the *NightHawk* crew having been reminded of Andrew's abilities. They weren't that stupid.

Toni went to her old bunk in a pleasant haze enhanced by the dreams of a rosy future and too much of Jonny's good wine.

Emotion: concern.

It's all right, Pumpkin. Everything is fine.

Emotion: uncertainty.

All right, Nzinga. You're the one who's sharp. You stay on guard. I have to sleep. I want to sleep. But I'm going to dream a while first.

Emotion: willingness to serve.

Toni drifted into a pleasant place where reality did not intrude.

The following morning she awoke and wondered, not for the first time, how humanity had survived for thousands of years without Juanita's *mañana siguiente* concoction. She didn't care. She staggered to the mess, where a large jug of the dark-green sludge sat on the counter with exactly the right sized glasses. She poured a dose and tossed the mixture back, sighing as the minty flavor cut through the fuzz on her tongue.

"Feels good, doesn't it?"

Her bleary eyes focused. Andrew, seated at the other table, raised his empty glass. "Mum gives me a certain latitude on special occasions. I almost needed this."

She controlled the silly smile that was trying to take over her face. "It does have its uses."

Toni felt a tug at her augment. *Toni, will you drop into the chart room when you have a moment?*

Toni frowned to herself. *Right away, ma'am.*

She looked at Andrew. "Did I do something I shouldn't have, last night?"

"Why do you ask?"

"Captain wants to see me."

He shrugged. "Sorry, I can't help. As far as I was concerned, you acted with complete decorum."

She sighed. "Sorry about that."

"I was rather disappointed, myself, but perhaps it's for the better. At the moment, at least."

"How very leaderly of you."

He raised his eyebrows. "Yes. I surprise even myself sometimes."

"Anyway, when the captain calls..." she pushed herself erect.

As she passed him, she couldn't help herself. She laid a hand on his shoulder.

He reached up and trapped it, looking up into her eyes. "This is going to be really great, isn't it?"

Her heart leapt, but she steadied herself and smiled down at him. "I think so."

His hand gradually relaxed, and she slipped free and headed up the slideway, her head spinning.

She hesitated in the chart room doorway. Natalia had her feet up. Two glasses and a bottle labelled "Scotch Whisky" graced the desktop beside them.

The captain gestured to the chair. "Have a seat."

Toni sat, regarding the bottle and glasses with suspicion. "You wanted to see me, ma'am?"

"Yes. Don't worry. Your auguar didn't crap on the carpet. This is just a little personal chat." She set out the glasses and poured.

Toni raised her drink in a silent toast and took a sip. She could rarely afford scotch, and this went down smoothly, with a smoky aftertaste. "Personal chats with the captain are usually far from little. What's up?"

"I just thought I'd ask how things are between you and Andrew."

Her heart sank. She took another sip to play for time, then glanced at the captain. No clue. "Um...we're getting along fine. As usual...?"

"That's not what I'm asking."

Toni set her glass carefully on the table. "I didn't think so."

"*Diablo* brought a lot of stuff out for us. Updates on personnel records, that sort of thing. I got around to looking at them."

"I see."

"Including some interesting test results."

Unnecessary to answer. The captain would get to her point when she was ready.

"Including a note from a Dr. Proust. The name is familiar?"

"I'm not surprised."

"So. Was the procedure successful?"

"It seems to have been."

"In what respect?"

"We have been able to readjust our relationship to maintain a professional distance while pursuing a personal friendship." She grinned wryly. "The guys who wrote the Space Arm training manuals would be proud of us."

"I see. And are you happy with that?"

Toni frowned. "Why wouldn't we be?"

"No, I'm asking you. Are you happy with that?"

"Of course I am." She sat straighter. "Captain, it's always been a damned rough job dealing with that kid. Now he's full-grown, built like a Commando training poster model and talks like he's thirty, which makes it even harder. You don't know what you're asking."

The captain took a slow sip, regarding her over the rim of her glass. "That wasn't my original intention."

"What wasn't?"

"I hoped you would bond, because then you would do a better job of protecting him. I didn't count on his maturity. Or your latest development." She put her glass down and leaned forward.

"Look, Toni, I'm sorry about this. When I took Andrew on I knew it would change my life. I had no intention that it would change yours."

Toni set her glass down as well and spread her hands on the table. "Wait a minute. Who says this has changed my life?"

"No, no, I'm not saying it has. I'm worried it could. I don't want this situation to hurt you in any way."

"But even more, you don't want it to hurt Andrew."

Natalia leaned back. "That's right. I'm glad you understand."

Toni relaxed and picked up her glass. "You don't have to worry about that. I could never do anything to hurt Andrew."

The captain had a strange smile on her face, as if she knew something she wasn't telling. "And why is that?"

"Because there are few opponents in this universe that I would rather not face than you, protecting Andrew."

Natalia burst out laughing.

"That wasn't meant to be funny, ma'am!"

The captain made an effort and controlled herself.

"Do you know why I sent you downplanet with him the day you met the barwolves?"

"Sure. You had all sorts of reasons."

Natalia shook her head. "Toni, one thing you learn to do as an officer is to make up all sorts of good reasons to tell your troops for doing what you want to or have to do."

"So, why did you send me downplanet with your son?"

"Because there are few opponents in the universe that I'd like less to come up against than you, defending Andrew."

"What?"

"Think about it. Your affection for him. Your protective instinct. Your loyalty to your cadre. Your loyalty to me. What you call your fear of me, which is just another way of saying your determination not to disappoint me. When I was sending Andrew into a dangerous situation, you were the ideal candidate for a guardian. Whatever happened after that, you earned yourself."

"You mean I got to where I am now because you thought I was a good babysitter?"

Natalia grinned. "Ain't life a bitch? And here you thought it was because you were so tough." She raised her glass.

Toni raised hers, and they drank.

"So, where does that leave us?"

The captain shrugged. "Nowhere. This was an idle conversation that has a lot to do with our friendship and little to do with the realities of life."

"Because…"

"Because the two of us sitting here deciding what is going to happen to Andrew is like two farmers talking about the rain."

"Ah. Andrew."

"That's right. Andrew will do what Andrew wants to do, and neither you nor I can stop him. And that's a warning as well. You have to think about yourself, here."

"Me?"

"Yes. The relationship you have with Andrew — friend, lover, lifetime companion, whatever — is going to depend a whole lot on where his life leads him. And no matter how that affects you, that is where he will go."

"I had considered that."

"Good. Glad we have that settled." The Captain poured again.

Toni took the glass and sipped, gazing at the image of the Barnard System stretched out across the viewscreen. It really was good whisky.

THE END

If you enjoyed this book, do the author and other readers a favour and go to your favourite retailer and post a review. Even a rating and a few words is great.

ABOUT THE AUTHOR

Brought up in a logging camp with no electricity, Gordon Long learned his storytelling in the traditional way: at his father's knee. He now spends his time editing, publishing, travelling, blogging and writing Fantasy, Sci-Fi and Social Commentary, although sometimes the boundaries blur.

Gordon lives in Tsawwassen, British Columbia, with his wife, Linda, and their Nova Scotia Duck Tolling Retriever, Josh. When he is not writing and publishing, he works on projects with the Surrey Seniors' Planning Table and is a staff writer for <indiesunlimited.com>

MORE FROM GORDON A. LONG

Other Titles by Gordon A. Long available at most retailers

"Factory 4-80" Freighty Series 1
"Outback Rebellion" Freighty Series 2

"Ocean of Grass" Petrellan Saga 1
"Waves of Stone" Petrellan Saga 2
"Path of Water" Petrellan Saga 3
"Zoysana's Choice" Petrellan Saga 4
"The Innkeeper's Husband" Petrellan Saga 5

"Out of Mischief" World of Change 1
"Into Trouble" World of Change 2
"Mountains of Mischief" World of Change 3
"The Trouble with Tents" World of Change 4
"Queen of Mischief" World of Change 5
"A Sword Called...Kitten?" Romantic Comedy with an Edge
"The Cat with Many Claws" Sword Called Kitten 2
"Cloud Cat" A Cat with Many Claws Novel
Storm Over Savournon (A Novel of the French Revolution)

"Why Are People So Stupid?" Social Humour with a Point

Look for Gordon's books, selected reviews, poetry and short stories: <airbornpress.ca>
Gordon's opinions on humanity are at the "Are People Stupid?" blog

Look for Gordon's books, selected reviews, poetry and short stories: <airbornpress.ca>

Gordon's opinions on humanity at the "Are People Really That Stupid?" blog: <https://airbornpress.ca/arepeoplestupid/>

Find all his reviews and his ideas on writing at "Renaissance Writer:" <https://airbornpress.ca/newdir/>